DISGUISED

Love

SANDRA MUZYKA

ISBN 978-1-7387154-9-7 e-book
ISBN 978-1-7387154-8-0 book

To John

Who always thought
my endeavours were
special.

Other Books
by
Sandra Muzyka

How to Make Money Flowers
Finding Thorold
Waiting for Santa
Pesky Bees
Lily and Tad
The Art of Expression
My Dog's Life
My Cat's Life
Carleton Falls

Chapter 1

"Get out and don't come back," Raye yelled as she slammed the front door after flinging his clothes on the front sidewalk. She had opened her heart to enough losers and was now at the end of her rope. She was done.

"How could I have been so blind as to get sucked in again," she cried as tears filled her eyes until they swelled, spilling over and over, again and again, like a leaky faucet. I really loved him and I thought he loved me too, she thought, as she placed the kettle on the stove and turned on the burner hoping a cup of peppermint tea would calm her nerves.

Raye sat down at the kitchen table waiting for the water to boil, sobbing breathlessly over kicking Steve out. She realized that he did want to be with her, but for all the wrong reasons, she was a shoo-in. He got home-cooked meals and a roof over his head. "What more could he ask for?" she asked herself, already knowing the answer.

"He had my heart too," she wailed in gut wrenching anguish, overpowering the sound of the boiling kettle whistling like a locomotive.

Raye stopped crying long enough to get up and grab herself a paper towel using it to blow her nose and wipe away the tears. Regaining her composure, she turned off the stove and poured the boiling water into her cup containing a peppermint tea bag. She was hoping the tea would relax her, but she knew what she really needed was a shot or two of whisky. But she and Steve had finished the bottle on their six-month anniversary, when he proposed to her. She didn't say yes because she explained to him that it was the first time she had been on her own and didn't want to get married just yet. After everything that had happened to her, she needed some time and told him to eventually ask her again. After all they were in love, living together and he knew they would eventually get married.

The nerve of him, she thought, as she tried to hold the tears back. Luckily, she didn't marry Steve when he had asked her. The thought of trying to get out of a marriage made her feel sick to her stomach. He would have ended up with money and maybe even property, her money and property, when he had nothing.

She sobbed into her tea thinking of what might have been. She needed to cry and get it all out. Raye didn't have a shoulder to cry on, no one to talk to, she had just kicked the only person in her life, out the door. She felt as if he had pulled at her heart strings and cut them with a blunt knife, separating any love she could now give to him or any man. She was now wounded and realized the only person she could rely on was herself.

Raye needed to control her emotions, or she would be back where she was a year ago, depressed, taking meds and not wanting to go on.

"I can't do it anymore," she blurted out sipping on her cup of tea as she looked over at Sidney sitting on the chair next to her giving her a sympathetic look. He was a tabby cat that she adopted, that had been hanging around the place when she bought it. He was a good listener and always came to Raye for affection. Sidney was good therapy for her and kept her grounded, plus he finally had someone to take care of him too. They were both alone and it made perfect sense to stick together.

"You didn't like Steve, did you? I should have listened to you Sidney." With each stroke she gave Sidney, Raye's mind focused on Steve, who had really been a stray too, she thought as she sobbed shaking her head, finally realizing the scum of the earth that he really was. The more she thought about Steve using her and the love she gave him, the more she had thoughts of seeing her parents for the very last time.

It was a dark and dingy night, and it had been raining all day. That morning Raye had gotten up to the smell of pancakes, syrup and homemade jam. Raye reminiscing how happy everyone was and her mom laughing at the old secondhand T-shirt Raye was wearing with the slogan . . . *Eat our beans and have the last word*. Raye smiled through her teary eyes thinking of how it was, longing to be home again with her mom and dad.

"I wish they were here right now," she said as she looked over at Sidney still patting his head.

The tears had stopped for a moment as Raye visualized her mom standing at the island turning over the pancakes and her dad sitting at the table letting her mom know he wanted his usual four stacked pancakes with a dollop of butter and a drizzle of syrup over top. They were a great team she thought as her mind fast forwarded to all of them getting into the car, leaving for…

Raye, reliving that morning, was startled, hearing a knock, knock, knock at the front door. The old, cast-iron door knocker was one of her favourite things about the house. She could hear it in any room sounding like a hammer hitting a piece of metal. She hoped it wasn't Steve wanting her to take him back, but she knew she would have to see him eventually as he still had a key to the front door. Raye walked down a hallway which led to the foyer, where she stood in front of a large floor mirror trying to fix her short bob hair style and pinching her cheeks hoping to make it look like she hadn't been crying, before answering the front door.

It is what it is, she thought as she saw a figure of a man through the lace curtain hanging over the large glass panel in the wooden door. She knew it wasn't Steve as the stature of the man was taller and bigger build than Steve. Thank goodness she thought, not wanting to put up with anymore of his nonsense.

As she opened the front door it creaked, the usual fix of cooking oil on the hinges hadn't seemed to work. Standing on the other side was a man maybe in his late thirty's she thought, carrying a suitcase and a duffel bag. He had dark brown hair and a few days of facial scruff.

"Are you Raye Daniels?" the man asked, then Raye giving him a nod in the affirmative. "I saw your ad in the local newspaper," he continued, as she gave him the once over. "I'm in-between jobs right now and was hoping you could use a handyman in exchange for one of your rooms to rent, plus two meals a day."

If it was one thing Raye didn't need right now was another man leeching off of her, but she did need some repairs done for sure. She had bought this large old house with seven bedrooms, five upstairs and two extra rooms with an ensuite on the main floor which she used as her bedroom and a den. Now, all the other rooms but one remained vacant. Early this morning she put an ad in the paper hoping to rent them out again. She had become the owner of a rooming house instead of a grand family home as it must have been many years ago.

Raye invited the man into the foyer so she could interrogate him.

"Your home is beautiful," he said very impressed and found it to be more of a stately mansion than just an old house. "The polished wooden wainscoting and vintage damask wallpaper is breathtaking and still in wonderful shape," he was telling Raye, like she hadn't noticed. "You just can't find ornamental mouldings like that anymore," he continued as Sidney had greeted him with a rub along his shin hoping the man would reciprocate with a petting. The man looking worn out and tired knelt down to pet Sidney as Sidney purred louder and louder from all the attention he was getting, which was a plus in Raye's eyes; him liking cats. She was going to make this a prerequisite for renting any rooms going forward.

Still petting Sidney, the man looked up at Raye. "Are you okay, I noticed you've been crying?"

"No," said Raye abruptly, not wanting to go into why she was upset. "It's just a bad case of seasonal allergies. I was outside weeding and ran into a few golden rods."

"I see," said the man, not knowing whether to believe Raye or not, as he got up from petting Sidney. "I can help with that as well. I have done some landscaping in the past. If you're not happy with my work or you don't think the work I'm doing is worth renting a room, you just have to say the word and I will leave."

Raye looked into his blue eyes trying to get a feel of his intent. "You seem to know a lot about architecture and design. What is your name, sir," she asked, still looking at him eye to eye.

"My name is Gage Manning," he said as Raye waited for him to say anything else to convince her to let him stay.

One thing for certain, she wouldn't have to worry about Steve trying to wheedle his way back in with another man in the house. That alone would be a plus for her and a good reason to let him stay. Steve always wanted the rooms rented to women. He had convinced her that men would be trouble. She now knew the reason why; it just made it easier for him to have relations with them and keep an eye on her as well. When she found Steve and two of her tenants in bed together, she told them to leave, or she would call the police. They packed their bags and left while she was getting rid of Steve and his belongings. Then she had to clean the rooms and put on fresh bedding.

With her blank stare into his eyes, Gage could see Raye in deep thought. "I can see you're not sure about me, Miss. I won't bother you any longer. Have a nice day," he said as he turned to leave.

"Wait, please," said Raye, knowing she had to rely on her instincts, which hadn't been good lately. Sidney and Gage liked each other, not like Sidney always running away from Steve. "I will show you to a room. You have four to choose from as one is already rented. It belongs to the woman who used to own the house. She spends most of her time abroad but keeps a room for when she comes home, which may be only once a month, if that."

A smile came to the man's face, as he gave out an exhale, calming his body, as he thanked Raye for hiring him.

"No need in thanking me, I will have a list of things for you to do tomorrow," said Raye as she led Gage up the elegant staircase to a room at the top of the stairs to the left. "This is one of the larger rooms, with a queen size bed."

Gage was just happy to have a bed to sleep in tonight. "Where is the bathroom?" he asked, hoping to take a nice hot shower.

"It's two doors down on the right with a tub and shower; it's a nice-size room too. The room that is rented is the back bedroom on the left and it has an ensuite as well. The door remains locked at all times. No one is to go in for any reason."

"I understand. This room here is perfect for me; I won't need to look at any others and again, thank you."

"No need, hopefully we can help each other. Dinner is at six. If you need to do any laundry there is a washer and dryer in the basement. I also have a clothesline in the side yard. As the rooms become filled, I will put up a schedule for specific laundry days. I'm sure you would like to get settled. I will see you later Mr. Manning."

"Thank you, please call me Gage."

"Of course, I will see you later Gage," said Raye as she left him and headed downstairs to the kitchen.

So far this has been an interesting day, it was already after one, better eat she thought and start a list, so Gage has something to keep him busy starting tomorrow. "First a ham and Swiss on rye, maybe I should make one for him too, since he really looked like he could use one," she said looking at Sidney following her into the kitchen. Dinner could wait for now, even though homemade stew would take some time preparing and cooking. While making the sandwiches Raye chopped up a slice of ham for Sidney. "Here you go Sid, enjoy your lunch, much better than dry food."

Raye put the plate with Gage's sandwich on a tray along with a glass of lemonade she had made the night before and carried it up the stairs to his room. She wasn't going to make this a habit, delivering meals, but looking so worn out she thought he could use a bite. Gage, not expecting Raye was coming out of the bathroom and down the hall with a towel wrapped around his waist. His body was muscular, his shoulders wide and his waist trim to the point of having a very noticeable six pack.

"I'm so sorry . . . I just thought . . . I . . . I don't know what I was thinking. I just thought you must be hungry," said Raye a little flushed and embarrassed. Besides his physique she couldn't help but notice he was clean shaven. He was definitely not as old as she thought he was. A clean shave made him a few years younger for sure.

Noticing Raye all flustered, he smiled. "That's okay, no harm done. Thank you for making this, I am pretty hungry," he said as he took the tray from Raye.

"You're welcome, nice seeing you," she said as she turned towards the stairway wanting to run down the stairs away from what just happened, to be anywhere in the house other than where she was. Raye, trying to regain her composure, went down the staircase shaking, hoping her legs would keep her up . . . nice seeing you, I can't believe I just said that, she thought, realizing she had just seen his perfect body. She didn't know why she was acting the way she was, maybe because he startled her, she never did like surprises even if they were good ones. With having men rent the rooms she would just have to get use to it she thought—oh poor Mrs. Willoughby when she comes to stay. Rethinking it, she would just have to let them know that bath robes were to be used instead of towels.

With everything that had just happened with Steve, she needed to take control of her life, and it started today; thinking of a list of jobs for Gage to do. She needed to stay focused on fixing the house and getting the other rooms rented.

Back in the kitchen eating her sandwich, Raye was making a list as she looked out the French doors into the backyard. Sidney had left the kitchen and was probably in the den lying on the wide windowsill basking in the sunshine coming through from the back of the house.

The backyard was a gardener's paradise with large curvy flower beds containing hydrangeas and azaleas spread throughout with lavender and rosy, red creeping thyme complimenting them. An old three-tier concrete fountain with an angel adorning it was the centerpiece of the yard with beautiful red rose bushes surrounding it. The fountain needed to be fixed which was on the list for Gage plus the weeds that were lodged between the slate patio stones. The large arbour over the patio also needed a support pole fixed. The wisteria, although beautiful, was overgrown and heavy which had weakened the structure.

Steve had complained about all the work that needed to be done but wouldn't lift a finger to help, which led

her to think about his escapades and shaking her head in
disgust.

Chapter 2

It was mid-afternoon as the warm sun beat down through a slight opening in the drawn curtains. After the tasty sandwich and nice hot shower Gage had fallen asleep on the soft comfortable bed. Hmm . . . a few more hours of sleep would be nice he thought as he rolled over, hearing a scratch at the bedroom door.

"I thought it was you, my furry friend," he said opening the door to let Sidney in. Sidney rubbing past him went for the cozy bedspread bundled up on the bed. "One second there, buddy, let me make the bed and then it's yours for awhile." Gage pulled the covers back picking up Sidney as he straightened the bedspread. "There you go, have a nice sleep," he said positioning the cat back on the bed.

Gage opened his suitcase and hung his shirts in the double closet. There was ample room and would accommodate two people nicely. The closet doors were made of oak as most of the doors throughout the house were. There was also a shelf to put hats or boxes on, so they were up off the closet floor. The walls were done in a beige vintage wallpaper and again large mouldings in their natural oak colour surrounded the ceiling and floor like the downstairs foyer. The floors were highly polished oak, and a large earth tone area rug covered most of the floor continuing under the bed. Two bedside tables with drawers were on either side of the spiral bed posts and a vintage stained-glass lamp on each. On the opposite wall of the bed was a wooden dresser with six drawers and a mirror plus a striped fabric chair in the corner beside the window. Gage continued to put some clothes into the dresser drawers leaving out a pair of jeans and a T-shirt that he slipped into. Unzipping a large pocket inside his duffel bag he reached in and pulled out a gun in its holster then opened a drawer on one of the bedside tables and placed it in. Once the suitcase and duffel bag were empty, he put them on the closet floor.

Maybe time to explore this house, he thought as he looked over at Sidney curled up in a ball. Gage opened his bedroom door and decided to look at the other rooms down the hall. There was more beautiful trim throughout with a hall runner leading the way. Peeking into the first door he opened; he saw a double bed nicely dressed with the standard chair and dresser. The colours of the room were gold tones but pretty much the same layout. Room number three was the same as the second room but done in a deeper beige than his room. The fourth room was a bit smaller than all the rest but everything one would need was there. This room was done in a very soft blue making it seem bigger than it actually was. Each door was closed to keep Sidney out he thought, as he moved on to the last room. The door was in fact locked as Raye had stated. Eventually he would get the key and have a look he thought, once he was on Raye's good side or when she thought she could trust him.

Gage went down the staircase to check out the main floor, carrying the tray Raye had given him. The formal living room was just that, very formal. The fireplace was definitely the focal point done in a beautiful marble mantle and surround with wooden bookcases on either side with stained glass doors which reflected the sunlight from the large front windows. The furniture again stayed with the old-fashioned turn-of-the-century décor. The large, framed painting hanging above the mantle was beautiful. The painting was of a man and a woman in a beautiful red hat dancing. Hmm . . . nice taste he thought as he looked over the other paintings in the room. "Are these copies?" Gage said to himself, noticing a sculpture sitting on the bookcase below the doors. Again, it looked liked an expensive artifact that should be in a museum along with the pottery sitting on the other bookcase.

"I see you have been exploring the house," said Raye, coming up behind Gage as he turned around to acknowledge her.

"It's a beautiful house and the way you've decorated it just makes everything more grand. I worked on my grandparents' home when I was a teenager. They wanted to restore a house they bought that was quite old too. Once we sanded the floors and a few coats of polyurethane, it brought them back to their original state. I'm wondering now why you wanted to hire me; your home is beautiful?"

"Thank you, but I can't take the credit. Mrs. Willoughby, who sold me the house also sold it with all the contents, except for certain items throughout the house that still belong to her. Plus, the agreement was that she had a room to come back to when she was in town. It was a perfect agreement for me and once I get those other rooms rented, I can get some money coming in."

Wanting to show Gage the rest of the house, Raye took him on a tour of the formal dining room which also had a fireplace as well as her bedroom plus ensuite and the room she made into a den. Off the hallway to the kitchen was a second closet that had been turned into a two-piece bathroom. The kitchen was her favourite place of all. The cupboards went to the ceiling and where traditional oak with cast iron handles. Through the French doors the view of the backyard was breathtaking. To enhance the kitchen Raye wanted to add an island and change the countertops. This is where some of the work was needed. She also wanted a copper hood above the antique stove which had already been purchased and in the basement just waiting for someone to install.

"I wasn't going to give you a list until tomorrow but maybe I should give you what I have as not to overwhelm you. I know it will take time, and I will constantly be adding things, I'm sure."

"That's fine," said Gage as Raye handed him the list. "I can get started on some of this now. Where are the tools kept, Miss Daniels?"

"Please call me Raye. Mrs. Willoughby's late husband had a workshop in the basement. You will find everything you need. It's through here and down the stairs," as Raye pointed to a doorway off the kitchen. "The light is on a pull chain just above the first step and another at the bottom of the stairs then again in the workshop."

Leaving Gage to explore the workshop Raye needed to get the stew started or she would have to prepare something else for dinner. First, she browned the stewing beef and chopped onions then added it to a pot with the drippings from the stewing beef. Next, she added some beef broth and her mixture of seasoning not forgetting a few glugs of red wine.

Raye stared into the pot stirring it, thinking back at how she and Steve had met in a wine store, both looking for the same brand of red wine. He had bumped into her, and they hit it off from the very beginning, then following her to Turnersfield, a small town away from big city life in Bryerton, Vancouver. Away from everything she had known. Thinking about what Steve had done she wondered if he had lied about anything else.

Raye, just wanting to get this day over with and have a good night's sleep drifted back to reality peeling and cutting the potatoes and carrots along with chopped celery, placing them into the pot, leaving the frozen peas to the end. "Mmm . . . smells good. Now to let it slow cook." she said adding the lid to the pot.

Her cell phone started ringing as she finished towel drying her hands. "Hello, yes this is. Tomorrow morning, that will be fine. Yes, see you then, bye." Raye was hopeful that another room would be rented tomorrow.

Gage came up from the basement with a toolbox in hand, looking over at Raye as she finished her phone call. "I will work on the hood tomorrow when the stove isn't being used. For now, I will check the leak in your ensuite, so you won't have to worry about it any longer."

"Thanks Gage, that would be great. It's been leaking for quite some time." Raye smiled, thinking how nice it is to have someone around that knows how to fix things, finally feeling like she had made a good decision. "I'll walk with you as I need some towels from the linen closet in the hallway. I keep extra towels for the rooms upstairs in here," explained Raye, as Gage too was keeping up with small talk waiting for Raye to finish collecting the towels and leave.

Gage entered Raye's bedroom closing the door slightly as not to be seen from the adjoining hallway. Noticing a jewellery box on the antique dresser he opened the lid and browsed through it; a diamond necklace with earrings to match plus a ruby broach in silver or white gold. "What's under here," Gage said to himself lifting up the velvet lined tray in the jewellery box while trying to watch for Raye coming back and checking on him. He saw a man and woman's wedding bands plus an engagement ring, all of very good quality. If the diamonds were real, they would be very valuable, he thought as he closed the box and looked around for anything else that would be worth a pretty penny. There were no paintings or prints hanging on the walls or family pictures on the dresser or bedside tables. Having done a pretty thorough search Gage went to fix the leak under the sink hoping to permanently remove the pail Raye had put under there.

Raye already upstairs, put the towels in the other rooms, each room having different colours so the renters wouldn't get their towels mixed up. Closing the last bedroom door and heading down the hallway Raye noticed Sidney coming out of Gage's room. "What have you been doing pretty boy, you like our new guest, don't you? Come on, let's go downstairs," she said as her cell phone started to ring again. "Hello, yes this is Raye. I did . . . I have two rooms left. Tomorrow afternoon, say around two. Perfect, see you then." Another person wanting to rent a room, how wonderful she thought. Amazing how things have changed in one day after kicking Steve out. He must have been the negative vibe throughout the house. Suddenly everything seemed much brighter, but she needed to get the key from him and didn't want to call him just yet.

Raye went to see how Gage was making out with her leaky sink. She could hear the sound of clanking pipes as she looked inside from the doorway. Gage was laying on his back reaching up under the sink while the rest of his body was sprawled on the floor with his T-shirt hoisted up from his waist. "How is it going, is it fixable?"

"It's an easy fix, can you hand me the vice grips please?"

Raye, not sure what vice grips were, handed him a wrench. "Close but not the right one. Could you hand me the other one that looks something like the one you just gave me?"

"Sure," said Raye, passing it to Gage as his hand touched hers trying to get a hold of it.

"Perfect, I will make you a handyman's assistant before you know it," said Gage as he tightened the hot water pipe. "I'm going to turn the shutoff valve back on. Could you please turn on the hot water tap?"

Gage made his way from under the sink. "You can turn it off now, there aren't any leaks, and you won't need the pail anymore."

"Thanks, that's great. Now it's one less thing to deal with. What's the next thing on your list for today?"

"Since they are calling for rain tomorrow, I thought I would check out the things you need done in the backyard. But first I want to fix the squeaky front door hinges. It's the first thing you hear coming into the house."

"I will leave you to it," said Raye with a smile, "see you for dinner at six in the dining room."

Raye went to the kitchen to check the stew; it was cooking nicely and had two hours of cooking time left which gave her enough time to take a bath in her antique claw foot tub. She turned on the water and put in some bubble bath. Raye undressed, taking off her sweatshirt and stepping out of her sweatpants. Her undergarments were now lying on the floor as she stepped into the tub, sinking into the abyss of warm, very warm bubble infused water. What a day she thought as she relaxed and closed her eyes.

Raye! . . . Raye! I'm coming in if you don't answer, yelled Gage on the other side of the bathroom door.

In a deep sleep dreaming about her parents, Raye could hear someone calling her name. "I'm okay . . . I guess I fell asleep. I'll be right out," she said as she slowly got up grabbing a towel before stepping out of the tub. All dried off she put on a bra and panties then a pair of leggings and a long off-the-shoulder top. She brushed her hair and put on a little blush, so she didn't look so pale.

As Raye headed to the kitchen, she saw the light on in the dining room and the table set. Gage was coming from the kitchen with a large bowl and some bread on a plate. "I'm so sorry Gage, what time is it?"

"It's six thirty. I was getting worried when you didn't answer. I knew you wanted to eat at six. Are you okay?"

"I'm fine and thank you for doing all of this," said Raye looking at Gage as she sat down to eat.

"I just set the table, you did the rest," Gage smiled as he passed her the bowl of stew, waiting for her to take the first spoonful. He couldn't wait to fill his plate as the aroma was so mouth watering. Taking his first bite, he then looked at Raye, "delicious," he stated, wiping his mouth with a napkin.

"I'm glad you like it, it's a family recipe," said Raye teary-eyed, sweeping the blonde hair off her brow.

Gage noticed that Raye seemed preoccupied and didn't want to ask her why unless she brought it up and wanted to talk. For now, he was the hired help and shouldn't ask any questions. The evening had resumed a flowing conversation even as they both cleared off the dining room table. A few laughs could also be heard as Gage told Raye about a couple he knew, that bought a restaurant but neither of them knew how to cook. They relied solely on one guy: their chef. He didn't speak English, so they were more frustrated on a daily basis trying to get him to understand. They all went through quite an ordeal until they decided to pay for the chef to learn how to speak English. In the end it all worked out.

Gage decided to help with the dishes as Raye went back to the dining room to get the glasses. Bringing them to the kitchen Raye misjudged the counter, and the glasses hit the floor shattering into a million pieces. Gage, surprised, turned around to see Raye standing there in limbo with a blank look, tears suddenly running down her face. She looked like a wounded animal; Gage thought as he put his arms around her and guided her to a chair at the kitchen table. "I'll clean up the glass," he said not knowing if she could even hear him, just staring off into her own little world. As he tried to pull away Raye hung on tightly not wanting to let him go. The cleanup could wait until she was ready, he thought as he sat down beside Raye giving her all the time she needed.

Chapter 3

"I deserve more and I'm going to get it. I didn't invest months of babysitting this broad just to help you out. You're going to help me get what I want little brother, or I will turn you in! Do you hear me?" yelled Steve determined to get what he wanted, and the old woman was his ticket.

"I know, I know, I said I'll do my share. I see your ex-girlfriend in an hour, and I'll rent a room."

"Make sure you use an alias; we can't let her know we're related. So far, she doesn't even know I have a brother," Steve said with a smirk and revenge in his eyes hoping to make Raye pay for throwing him out.

His plan was to marry Raye and get half of the insurance money she received from her parent's death. The family home being on the north side of the city also sold for a lot of money, making Raye financially stable. But the real money was inside the old woman's locked room. When she came home to stay for a while she and Steve had gotten to know each other. She never had any children and became very fond of Steve. She had told Steve she didn't like to put all her eggs in one basket and needed a safe to keep her valuables in. She trusted Steve enough to confide in him, letting him know she had bought a safe and was having it delivered. He was the one who carried it up the stairs and bolted it to the floor for her. It was the only good deed he did for a perfect stranger all the while knowing he would some day steal from her. Now the only thing that stood in his way was Raye.

Steve, looking back at his plan, knew it would have worked. Raye never knew him bumping into her at the wine store was a set up. All he had to do was make her fall in love with him and marry her for the insurance money. Angrily, he walked back and forth nodding his head thinking about how she screwed up his plans by throwing him out. Furious, at this point he turned to his brother pointing his finger. "You just remember what's at stake here!"

"Don't you think I know?" Parker said in anguish over the thought of what he had done. One drink too many and a bad night for driving was his only defense but no one heard it because of big brother figuring out a way he could benefit from little brother's misfortune.

Parker threw his backpack over his shoulder and picked up his duffel bag as he gave one last look at Steve. "See you, bro, I'll call you later to let you know what happened." Then he walked out the door hoping Steve's plan would work.

Parker was three years younger than Steve, and they pretty much raised themselves. Their dad had left their mother when Steve was six and he always felt responsible for Parker. At age eight their mother took off with a man and never came back leaving the boys to fend for themselves. The owner of the building found out they were alone. He wanted them out of the apartment, so he called child welfare, and they became permanent wards of the government where they remained until Steve became of an age to work and take care of Parker.

Parker turned on his car wipers as the rain was coming down pretty fast. The address was on the outskirts of town and the gloomy day reminded him of that night. It was always on his mind as Steve wouldn't let him forget it. The rain had stopped as Parker turned the corner continuing down the road looking for 17 Terry Lane. It was the last house sitting by itself nestled within large oak and sycamore trees. "Wow, is this the right place?" Parker muttered as he slowed down pulling into the driveway. "Steve wasn't kidding, it just reeks of money."

Parker got out of the car making his way to the front door leaving his bags in the car, not wanting to make it look like he was eager to rent. Placing his hand on the door knocker he knocked a few times, waiting for a response.

The large wooden door opened and a young woman standing on the other side said hello. "Hello, are you Raye Daniels? I called about your ad for renting a room," said Parker as he gave Raye the once over.

"Yes, if you would like to come in, I will show you the rooms. What's your name?" Raye asked, looking him over and remembering about Sidney.

"My name is Parker Cleve, and I have a steady job in construction, so you won't have to worry about me paying my bill."

"I have a cat Mr. Cleve, do you like cats? Oh, here is Sidney." Raye chuckled as if Sidney had come right on cue.

"Yes, I don't mind cats," said Parker greeting Sidney with a rub on the head and Raye watching closely.

"I'll show you the rooms available Mr. Cleve and if you want to stay here, I will gladly rent a room to you," said Raye as she led the way up the staircase.

"Please call me Parker and I'm sure the room will be fine," he said taking in his surroundings and the elegance throughout the house.

Raye told him there was a man staying in the first room on the left and she showed him a room on the right with a double bed which Parker said would be fine. Raye asked for payment and said he was to pay weekly for the room. She also explained that he was renting the room for himself and not others. If he had lady friends, he wasn't to bring them here in the house or in his room for any reason. It was a room to hang his hat and sleep and nothing more.

Handing him a piece of paper with all the conditions, he signed it, and she then handed him a key to his room. Having explained all the rules, she then explained about sharing the bathroom and to be courteous to other people renting a room. She also told him about the washer and dryer in the basement. His rent would not include meals as he wanted to fend for himself but if he wanted to eat in the dining room he was welcomed to do so. Parker always went to a pub style restaurant for his meals with the guys after work. He wasn't interested in home cooked meals.

They both walked to the stairway happy with the agreement. Reaching the bottom of the stairs Raye turned to Parker and smiled. "I hope you enjoy your stay, Parker and please call me Raye. If there is anything you need, please don't hesitate to ask."

Parker thanked her and continued through the foyer to the front door. Once outside he went to his car to retrieve his bags then returned to the house. Sidney greeted him at the top of the stairs and went into the room with Parker watching him put away his clothes.

"Okay furball, I don't mind cats, but we're not going to be best friends, now get!" Parker said in a raised voice, waving his arms scaring Sidney out of the room and down the stairs. Closing the door Parker took out his cell phone to call Steve. So far everything was going according to plan.

"I'm in Steve, she likes me. Our room is the first one on the right. There is a guy renting the room across the hall from me and she has someone coming to look at another room this afternoon. I will keep you posted." Parker could relax now knowing Steve would handle everything from here on in.

Closing the door behind him and locking it Parker went down the staircase, now taking a look into each of the rooms. He had never seen anything like it, upper-class for sure he thought, as he moved from room to room ending up in the kitchen.

"You must be the new guy," Gage said as he looked up, seeing Parker coming through the doorway. Exchanging names, they got a little more acquainted as Gage had asked him to help hold up the hood above the stove so he could tighten the bolts.

"You just saved me some time, thanks for the help."

"No problem . . . well, I need to get to work. I suppose we will be running into each other from time to time," said Parker as he turned to exit the room and Gage giving him a nod. Parker went down the hallway to exit the front door and saw Raye coming his way.

"Everything okay, Parker?" Raye smiled hoping all of the tenants would get along or if anything, just be pleasant to each other.

"The room is great and I'm going to work, I told them I wouldn't be too late. Does this key work for the front door as well just incase I'm late some nights?"

"No, the door stays unlocked until eleven and if you are later than that you just need to knock. I will hear it. But the agreement has a curfew, and should you make it a habit of being past eleven then you would have to leave. If you would like to change your mind please say so now, as I have other people interested."

Steve wasn't wrong, what a bitch he thought as she explained more rules. "No, I'm usually tired after a hard day's work. It won't be a problem," he smiled and nodded reassuring Raye he would abide by all the house rules. He had to or Steve would report him.

"Have yourself a good day." Raye smiled, now wondering if she had made a wise choice. Time would tell, she thought as she went into the kitchen to talk to Gage. She felt bad about what happened last night and needed to explain her behaviour.

"Good morning, I thought I heard some work being done." Looking at the copper hood above the stove Raye couldn't believe her eyes. "It looks so beautiful Gage. Thank you so much, you did a great job. What a difference it makes in the kitchen."

Gage smiled. "I'm glad you like it and good morning to you too. The new guy helped hold it. It was good timing really otherwise it would have taken me a lot longer."

"I'm very pleased, now I just have to pick out some new countertops," Raye chuckled waiting to see Gage's reaction.

"Just let me know when and I will have these countertops removed the day before their delivery."

"I will let you know for sure. Gage, there is something else I would like to talk to you about. I really appreciate what you did for me last night and the mess you cleaned up."

"That's quite all right you don't have to explain," Gage insisted, trying to stop her from explaining. "It's really none of my business."

"I need to because it will happen again and again, I can't control it, but I do remember what happened last night and you were so kind to stay with me. About a year ago I lived with my parents in Bryerton. One particular night we went to see a concert that we had bought the tickets for months in advance. They were very hard to get, and we were anxious to go. It had been raining all day and was still raining on the way home." Raye's voice becoming low and shaky looked away from Gage staring into the distance.

"Coming home we were hit head on by what they thought was a flatbed or pickup truck because of the damage that was done to the front of the car. My parents never had a chance. I was told two men passing by saw smoke coming from the car and pulled me out. They got me to safety before it was engulfed in flames. The driver crossed the center line and headed straight for us and got away with it. I wondered for a long time why I survived, and I wished I hadn't," Raye said as her green eyes became tear filled showing Gage just how emotionally hurt she was. "The doctors told me until my brain deals with the trauma I went through; the flashbacks won't go away. My brain is trying to figure it out, piecing it all together. I don't remember a lot about what happened, but my brain is showing me in its own way. Sometimes I relive the nightmare over and over again in my sleep, hearing my mother calling out to me for help."

Gage felt sorry for Raye and realized what a terrible thing she had gone through. He could see she was very vulnerable and expressed his sympathy. "I'm so sorry for your loss and what you are going through. Hopefully they catch the person who did it. Why didn't you stay in Bryerton?"

"I had to get away and hoped moving here would be better for me. I was an ER nurse, and my flashbacks were affecting my job. I would break down and cry when someone would come in with a bloody head or face. It would send me right back to the crash seeing the smashed windshield and my mother calling me. I couldn't get to her. The next thing I remember was being in the hospital. I cried for days and wanted to end my life, so they sedated me. I just wanted to be with them, and I didn't know why I was spared." Her eyes widened as she looked at Gage thinking she had told him enough and not even wanting to mention her ordeal with Steve.

"Some things just take time, I'm sure you will get through this," said Gage giving her all the assurance she needed.

"Thank you for understanding, Gage, I appreciate it. I will leave you to finish up, I have a few errands to run and will be back after lunch. I left a sandwich and some cut up fruit in the refrigerator for you." Raye with a smile left the kitchen and gathered her coat and car keys.

The sun was peeking through the clouds drying up the rain that had fallen earlier. Raye needed to buy dry food for Sidney and enquire about countertops at the local hardware store. They also sold ready-made islands, but they weren't as big as Raye wanted. Once inside the store she decided to go with bottom cupboards and put at least four together side by side. This way she would have a lot of storage too. Now she needed to have the cupboards delivered and they could measure for the new countertops as well. Raye, happy with her finds, could finally see her kitchen coming together.

Chapter 4

The hinges on this door needed to be oiled too; Gage thought as he opened the door and closed it behind him. If it's one thing he didn't want, it was Raye to find out he took the key for the locked bedroom. He didn't know how long she would be, so he needed to move quickly.

It was definitely the nicest room and the biggest, having a sitting area with beautiful antique furniture. Another beautiful painting hung on the wall as Gage attentively inspected the signature. Not a copy for sure as he carried on looking through the room. Opening the closet door he noticed a pull chain light. Turning it on he discovered a large safe in the corner, bolted to the floor. This should be interesting he thought, pondering the idea of opening it. He had cracked a few safes before but didn't have time and most of all didn't want to get caught. He would definitely have to open it before Mrs. Willoughby came home. Turning the light off and closing the closet door he went over to the side window noticing the driveway below. He saw Raye pull in and another car with a man standing along side of it. Gage quickly left the room making sure he locked the door behind him. Running down the staircase, Gage was able to put the key back on the hook he got it from as Raye entered the front door.

"Hello Sidney, this is Mr. Culpepper, Mr. Myles Culpepper to be exact and this is our resident cat, Sidney."

"Oh . . . you just call me Myles, luv, and I'll call you Raye, no formalities here."

"I couldn't agree more, Myles." Raye smiled as Sidney came right up to Myles.

"He's a beautiful cat, here kitty, kitty—oh—oh my." Sidney, not shy, climbed up Myles' pant leg landing in his arms. As Myles petted Sidney, he gave out a loud roar that made his eyes squint and his cheeks expand towards his eyes as his mouth turned upwards in laughter. "You and I are going to be great friends, Sidney."

Raye knew he was a very nice man and a good fit for her rooming house. "I'll show you the two rooms I have left, Myles. I'm glad I pulled in when I did otherwise you would have been waiting."

"At my age, you're not in a hurry anymore. I would have taken a seat in your backyard and enjoyed the scenery," smiled Myles as he climbed the staircase with Raye and Sidney following close behind.

Raye showed him the larger of the two rooms which Myles was happy with. He liked to paint and the light coming from that side of the house was perfect. "Your house is beautiful Raye, I'm sure I will be happy here. If it wasn't for my Louisa passing away and her taking out a second mortgage, I might have been able to stay in our home. I didn't know we were in so much debt as she took care of the finances. She did belong to a few charities, and she always liked to help others. I guess that's what I loved about her the most. Then when she got sick, the bills accumulated even more. I wanted her to have the best care around the clock, everything to make her comfortable. After she passed, I had no choice but to sell the house to pay bills. I'm just lucky I found your ad in the paper." Myles seemed overwhelmed and just needed to know where he would be for the rest of his years. He signed Raye's form and was happy to have found her.

"I'm glad you're here, Myles and I know we will get along very well. Lunch is at twelve and dinner is at six in the dining room and a small bar fridge in your room will be fine. I will have Gage; my handyman come and talk to you, and he can help you with that. I will also ask him to help you with your luggage. The stairs can be a little exhausting. You're also welcome to spend time in the living room as well as the backyard. This is your home now, so please enjoy your time here." Raye had a good feeling about Myles. He felt like a grandfatherly type or maybe it was the slight British accent either way he would definitely look out for Sidney.

Myles went to get his luggage from his car and Raye went to talk to Gage about helping Myles get settled. Raye knew those two would hit it off. They were both down to earth considerate people, now wondering even more about Parker; if he will be a good fit. We will see she thought as she went to get her phone from the table in the front hallway. The ringtone was set loud; a good thing otherwise she might have missed the call.

"Yes, now is a good time, I will see you in a bit, bye." One room to go, filling it will make a full house. No women had called which she thought strange, but she would have declined any knowing she already had three men. After Steve and his escapades, young women weren't even going to be considered.

"Here let me get the door," seeing Gage and Myles with their hands full. "Are you sure that room is going to be big enough?" chuckled Raye watching Myles carrying three wooden cases and a folded easel under his arm. "These are my babies, can't let anything happen to these, Miss, I would be very gutted if I lost them."

Hmm . . . he must mean upset, thought Raye knowing she would be hearing other British words, smiling to herself as the guys went up the staircase to Myles' room. Raye was still in the foyer and a possible tenant looking for a room was knocking at the front door. "Come in, I'm Raye and you are?" Raye asked hoping to rent the last room.

"Nice meeting you Raye, I'm Finch Edwards. I'm a first-year university student and need to rent a room during the school year. When I saw your ad, I knew I had to act on it. The school year will be starting soon which means rooms everywhere will be gone and student rooms by the university can be very pricey."

Raye thought he was a well-spoken young man and down to earth. His sandy brown hair and big hazel eyes gave him that boy-next-door look. She just had to smile and nod as he was pretty much telling her his life story. He was a nice young man from a little town called Fir Falls in Calgary. This was his first time away from home and he was given the name Finch because it was his mother's maiden name. It was a perfect name since he was an avid bird watcher and enrolled in this university because of its Ornithology course, the scientific study of birds. Now Raye was wondering if she was going to become a babysitter rather than his landlord. She stopped him in the middle of describing the rest of the school courses he was taking; to let him know he should look at the room first as it was the smallest. If he wasn't happy with it, then there was no need to tell her anymore.

He followed her up the staircase and was immediately met by Sidney at the top of the stairs. He had followed Myles and Gage and was now curious as to this new person.

"This is Sidney, Finch, do you like cats?" Raye somewhat hoping this would be a deterrent for Finch.

"I love cats, in fact I have one at home, and his name is Ollie. He came to us as a stray and never left. I will miss him, but Sidney can keep me company whenever he wants." Finch, getting a little teary eyed talking about Ollie followed Raye to the vacant room. "This is perfect; all I need is a desk to do my homework on."

Raye, remembering the desk she had put in the basement, told Finch that he could use it, and he could help Gage bring it up. Signing the contract Raye told Finch the house rules along with lunch and dinner being served at twelve and six. Since he was going to be at school for lunch, she would make him a sandwich to take. Raye was getting good prices for her rooms and making two meals a day was okay with her. She wanted to provide a service and wanted them to feel at home. Myles was in his room getting settled as Gage was coming out. Raye introduced Finch to both Gage and Myles as Sidney squeezed between them heading for Myles' bed.

Raye stood back watching all of them getting acquainted. This was her new family now she thought all the while knowing they would eventually leave, and others would come in their place. Raye left them and headed to the kitchen to get dinner started. Tonight was going to be interesting having three men around the dining room table. Something special she thought, maybe a meat and potato meal with vegetables. Hmm . . . she had picked up ribs on sale and maybe baked potatoes were in order with a side of coleslaw. Under the counter in a drawer was a large stock pot that Raye filled with water. She wanted to boil the ribs before putting them into the oven to bake.

Gage and Finch had headed to the basement to bring up the desk. Raye could hear Finch talking Gage's ear off about being here. Reaching the top of the stairs Raye looked over at Gage and smiled. Nothing seemed to irritate Gage, taking everything in stride. It was a nice quality she thought as she cleaned the potatoes and wrapped them in tin foil.

Watching them carry the desk through the kitchen she remembered how heavy it was, "made of solid wood," her dad said when he brought it in the house for the first time, after her mom bought it. Raye had it since grade school and straight through university. Many great essays were written on that desk and many great neck massages were given to her by her dad as she was working. He would come in and tell her not to work too hard. "Even great thinkers needed a break now and then," he would say. Raye closed her eyes hoping to hear his voice, sounds she longed to hear and his warm embrace she always felt before she left for work with a kiss on the forehead. Tears began running down Raye's face wishing she could see her parents one more time.

"Are you okay?" asked Gage entering the kitchen seeing her in an emotional state. Without thinking he put his arms around her and gave her a hug and told her it would be all right. Not resisting Raye felt calm and safe, never having felt that way in Steve's arms. Steve always told her that a lot of people go through more than what she went through and to get over it. They're gone and your crying isn't going to bring them back, so grow up!

"I'm better Gage, thanks for being there, I appreciate your kindness and understanding," said Raye, as Gage let go of his embrace and leaned back against the counter.

"Anytime, if a hug can help you through this, then by all means. You're grieving in your own way, and your brain is processing what happened. You just need more time."

"Gage is right," said Myles as he was standing in the kitchen doorway. "I assume you are missing someone who is no longer with us."

"Yes Myles, my parents. They both died in a car crash, and I was spared," Raye said slowly lowering her head down not letting Myles see the tears forming in her eyes.

Myles went over to her and put his arm around her shoulders. "What gets me through missing my Louisa is remembering the happy times. The pain of losing someone will lessen as time goes on. They will always be there whenever you need them, they hear you, luv, and now you have a new family." Myles lifted Raye's chin to look into her teary green eyes. "Just enjoy us for as long as we are in your life. We have all come together for a reason. The length of time being here is not up to us; just enjoy today and every other today going forward."

Raye gave Myles a hug and thanked him for being so kind. He in turn said if she ever needed to talk that he was a good listener. Nodding her head she looked at Myles and Gage with a half smile and thanked them both for helping her through this. She would definitely lean on them if she needed to, which made her feel safe.

Gage and Myles went out the French doors to the backyard leaving Raye to finish her cooking. Myles couldn't wait to paint outdoors with Raye's yard being so picturesque. He went and got his sketch book, sitting there sketching as Gage was putting in a new pole to keep the arbour supported in strong winds. The odd jobs on the list were becoming less and less but he was beginning to see things that needed to be done as well, like the shed needing some paint.

Next on his list was tackling the fountain. He was hoping the tube was just plugged with dirt or it needed a new pump. Gage cleaned each tier and filled the base with water. The only thing left was to turn it on and hope for the best. The pump was working but not like it should, the water was dribbling out which meant it was plugged. Gage turned the pump off and took the garden hose to clean any debris stuck in it. It didn't take Gage long and he got the fountain working. What a beautiful sound of trickling water, even Myles looked up from his drawing to see its beauty.

"Time to eat guys," called out Finch, eager to have his first home cooked meal away from home. "The fountain looks great," he yelled giving both Myles and Gage a thumbs up. Heading back through the kitchen to the dining room Raye was already seated at the head of the table. The food smelled delicious, and Raye directed

Finch to his place at the table wanting Gage to have his usual spot.

"You out did yourself luv, it smells wonderful," said Myles choosing his seat at the table, next to Finch. Myles was the first to take some ribs and passed them along to Gage. Finch grabbed a baked potato and cut it open adding shredded cheese, tomatoes and green onions that Raye had individually put into bowls, then adding a dollop of sour cream.

Raye looked up from her plate smiling; the men were concentrating on the ribs. She couldn't believe how quiet three men could be; even Finch was quiet enjoying the meal. Raye figured she would start a conversation and mentioned how nice it was to have the fountain working again. She also mentioned there were more ribs in the oven. Yep, that did it. It was all about the ribs. Gage said they were the best he had ever tasted, and Myles agreed with Gage while Finch said if all her meals were as tasty as this he would never go home again. Raye figured she would just have to wait and let one of them start a conversation, until then just enjoy the three hungry men: her new family.

Chapter 5

It was getting late, and everyone was in their allotted rooms. Raye had made a cup of herbal tea and headed to her den to read a new book she had purchased in town. Her den was a cozy little room that she had furnished with things from her home back in Bryerton. It contained a cozy little loveseat and a matching floral chair sitting opposite each other with an antique trunk being used as a coffee table. A beautiful plush beige and red carpet grounded the whole room with bookcases on either side of the bench window seat under the large window. Beautiful mint green curtains adorned the top of the window and flowed down halfway on either side giving a very elegant look to the room. This was Sidney's favourite room in the whole house, fast asleep on the wide windowsill as usual.

Raye, getting comfortable put her feet up, then taking a sip of her tea; she opened up the book titled *The Ghost at Glennhill Mansion* and started to read chapter one.

The night air was brisk and damp as the rain fell gently to the ground in a hypnotic beat. Jess got out of the cab and placed her suitcase on the sidewalk in front of a grand stately old house built of stone, with a wrap around porch hugging its structure, protecting it from unwanted visitors.

Jess carried her suitcase and climbed the wooden stairs, walking across the narrow floorboards of the front porch to the elegant front door. There she stood in front of a huge oak door, feeling alone and nervous at the prospect of meeting her distant cousins. She pressed the button at the side of the door buzzing her presence.

The door opened slowly as a short bald-headed man with a crooked half smile greeted her. "You must be Jess; we have been waiting for you. Please, come in."

Jess nodded and carried her suitcase into the house and removed her damp scarf. "Cousin, Charles?"

"Yes, that's right, here; let me take your suitcase, Eleanor is waiting for us in the living room."

As Jess entered the living room, she noticed the elegant furnishings which came alive in the light from the blazing fire. Above the mantel was a very large picture of her grandfather, his piercing eyes staring down at her, making her feel quite uncomfortable. Jess had never met him but had seen pictures of him in the family photo albums.

"This is our cousin, Jess," Charles said, introducing her to Eleanor as she got up from her chair.

"We are glad to have you," Eleanor replied. "Will you be staying long?"

"Just a few days. Just long enough to get acquainted with both of you and Cousin Henry. Bye-the-way, where is Cousin Henry?"

Charles gave Eleanor a knowing look for just a second, and then replied, "Henry had to leave unexpectedly, he should return before you have to leave. You must be tired from your long journey, let me show you to your room."

Hearing the chimes of her old mantel clock sitting on the bookcase shelf Raye lifted her head to see the time. It was eleven, time to lock up for the night. Putting her feet on the floor she placed the book on the loveseat beside her. A crack of thunder jarred her nerves as she heard the driving rain hitting the windowpane, disturbing Sidney from his sleep. It's going to be a nasty night, she thought as she made her way to the foyer. Coming through the front door was Parker, all wet from the downpour and smelling like a brewery. The wind had picked up making it hard to close the front door. He slammed it shut and turned the latch to lock it.

Parker, noticing Raye, swayed back and forth as he approached her, sending her backwards into the wall, knocking a picture to the floor. "Good evening, Raye," he said in a raspy tone, slurring his words. "I'm home just in time before curfew. How about you and I having a little drink together?"

"Parker, I think you need to go to bed and sleep it off," said Raye, upset at the broken glass while struggling to regain her composure at his lack of respect.

As Parker moved closer to Raye, Gage walked up behind him and grabbed his arm twisting it behind his back. "Come on, time for bed," he said escorting Parker up the stairs still in an arm hold.

"Hey man, I didn't mean any harm, let go!" Parker wailed trying to get free, just making Gage use a little more force pulling his arm even tighter behind his back. "Give me your key, Parker."

Parker, using his free hand pulled it out of his pocket and handed it to Gage. Once the door was open Gage pushed Parker onto the bed. "Sleep it off and apologize to Raye in the morning and if it ever happens again, I will throw you out. Do you hear me?"

Myles and Finch could hear him loud and clear as they stuck their heads out of their doorways to see what was going on. Parker, oblivious to much of what Gage said went to sleep, not disturbing anyone else. The other two closed their bedroom doors as Gage headed downstairs to find Raye.

Raye kneeling on the floor slowly picking up the pieces of glass, looked up at Gage. "I seem to always be thanking you. I don't know what I would have done if you hadn't stepped in," she said, now looking down at the glass in a sadden state.

Gage reached down, helping Raye get up from the floor. "It was just the booze talking, a little louder than most. He should be in bed for the night," Gage said looking into her eyes. "I will clean this up, it should be the handyman's job, remember."

Raye smiled as a large crack of thunder shook the house and threw her into Gage's arms. Gage feeling her warm body against his couldn't resist holding her tight. The lights flickered off and on, then another big crack of thunder with flashes of lightning illuminating the house. The house was now in total darkness as Raye held on even tighter to Gage. Gage still holding Raye brushed his lips on her forehead giving her a kiss then telling her to stay put until he came back with a flashlight.

Raye stood in place not knowing where the glass was, breathing deeply to everything that had transpired. Her eyes starred into the darkness with flashes of lightning radiating through the windows hypnotizing her back to her half-conscious state during the night of the accident with the streetlights reflecting a truck passing by. Raye stood there in disbelief then realized she saw something the night of the accident or was her mind playing games?

"I see you," said Gage shining the flashlight on Raye. "Be careful as not to step—are you okay, what's going on?"

"I just realized that I saw the truck that killed my parents. It drove past our car; it was a white truck. I saw it Gage, I saw it. Why didn't I remember that?" Raye in tears clung to Gage again wondering what else her mind was keeping from her.

Gage put his arms around Raye making her feel secure. "Your mind will eventually sort it out, you just need more time," he said, giving Raye all the reassurance she needed. "I don't think the lights will be coming back on any time soon. Maybe a good time to go to bed Raye and I'll clean up the mess so Sidney doesn't walk in it. Is this picture anything important?"

"No, just something I picked up in town."

"Then I won't worry too much about it. It looks like it's scratched quite a bit. Here's a flashlight, have a good sleep, Raye; everything should be back to normal tomorrow. We can talk more in the morning if you want."

"I am tired, you're right I could use a good sleep. Thanks again Gage," Raye said as she left him to clean up, her mind feeling so confused.

Raye went to bed thinking of what had just happened. She tossed and turned having a restless sleep always envisioning the car crash, her mind continuously trying to tell her something. Finally falling into a deep sleep, she awakened to the sound of a squeaky toy on her bed. It was Sidney's favourite furry mouse. "Good morning, pretty boy," said Raye reaching over to pet Sidney. The squeaky toy wasn't the only thing she heard.

There were noises and laughter coming from the kitchen. Raye getting up, put on her housecoat, then went to the bathroom to wash and fix her hair. The laughter and noise from the kitchen were getting louder, as she approached the kitchen door. Standing in the doorway she saw Gage, Myles, and Finch making breakfast. They had completely taken over her kitchen. Gage was cooking bacon and eggs; Myles was making waffles and Finch was on toast. Each was laughing and pointing at what they had made claiming they were the better cook. The laughter subsided as they saw Raye standing there smiling.

"Good morning, Raye," they all pretty much said in unison. "We wanted to surprise you luv," said Myles.

"Yes, and we wanted to let you know that you can count on us when needed," Finch jumped in. "Gage told us everything."

Raye, smiling, looked at the two guys. "Thank you, this is a very nice surprise, and everything smells wonderful," she said, then focused her eyes on Gage. "My handyman seems to be handy at a lot of things, thank you, Gage."

The kitchen table was set and a vase of fresh cut flowers from the garden was the center piece. They had thought of everything to make it a special day for Raye. They all sat around the table talking and laughing while eating their breakfast. It was more like brunch as the time was getting on. Even Sidney came for a piece of bacon that Raye had crumbled onto a plate beside her feet.

The conversation had stopped as they all watched Parker come towards the table. Steve had called him this morning and gave him a going over. "Why didn't you answer your phone, last night?" Parker told him he got in late and went to bed. Steve knew exactly what Parker was like. "You got drunk, didn't you? If you screw things up, I'll turn you in. You better make this right, do you hear me, make it right!" Those words echoed in Parker's head knowing what he had to do.

"Grab a plate and help yourself, Parker," said Gage waiting for an apology to Raye.

"Thanks, I need to get to work, but I would love a coffee and Raye, I owe you an apology for last night. It won't happen again." Raye smiled and thanked him for saying that. Parker knew he had to keep his nose clean for the rest of his stay. He made his coffee while everyone introduced themselves. He couldn't have been less interested as he had no use for them. If it hadn't been for Steve devising a plan to hide his work truck used in the crash as being stolen, Parker would be serving time which Steve had constantly reminded him. Parker left the group with his coffee in hand happy to be away from them.

The rest of them were really getting acquainted. Raye hadn't had this kind of chatter in the morning in a long time. She told them how she wanted to make a big island with stools in the center of the kitchen, which reminded her that the delivery from the hardware store would be coming this afternoon with the cupboards she had ordered, and they would then take measurements for the countertops she had picked out.

Gage looked over at Raye as Myles was telling her about his wife and the little things she used to do for him, Raye smiling and looking happy for a change. He was glad to see that and realized just what a pretty smile she had and how her green eyes glistened in the sunshine coming through the French doors. Her short blonde cut was a little boyish looking, but it complimented her cute freckled face, something that was becoming more irresistible to Gage. He couldn't let that persuade him and his reason for being there in the first place. He needed to stick to the plan and make Raye feel comfortable with his presence. He needed to open that safe and see what fortune lay inside before Mrs. Willoughby returned home. Now with three other people in the house it was going to be harder grabbing the key and entering the room unnoticed.

The men cleaned up the kitchen as Raye went to shower and get dressed for the delivery guys coming. The morning flew by, and it was already two o'clock. Myles was outside painting and Finch left to explore what would be his new campus and the new town he had become a part of. Turnersfield had a lot of history, more than most small towns. They even had a small museum that Mrs. Willoughby and her late husband were curators of The Turnersfield Fine Arts Museum.

"I'll get it!" Gage yelled out to Raye, hoping she could hear him. "Hi, the kitchen is this way." Gage pushed the kitchen table against the wall giving the guys a little more room to set down the cupboards.

"Two more to go then we'll measure the counters."

"Great, I will let her know you're here," said Gage going to check on Raye and why she hadn't heard him. Her bedroom door was slightly ajar, probably to let Sidney come and go. He saw her standing there putting on her clothes not wanting to disturb her. It had been a long time since he was in a relationship and her body was very enticing. The clothes she wore were very deceiving he thought, as she had a beautiful figure, very alluring. Not wanting her to see him watching her he knocked on the door. "Raye, the men with the cabinets are here."

"I'll be right there," she said pulling her sweater over her head not noticing that Gage had been standing there all that time. Finally dressed, she made her way to the kitchen.

"Thank you so much, the cabinets look great, would you mind lining them up for me right here then you can take a measurement for the countertop with an overhang." The men followed Raye's direction and got all the measurements needed. They told her it would take a week, and they would be delivered in the afternoon. Gage took notice of the day as he would have to remove the old countertops the day before so they could install the new ones.

Gage walked them out as Raye admired the cabinets. All that was needed was screwing them together and painting them. The height was perfect with so much more storage.

"You made a good decision," Gage stated, looking them over. "I'll go get my tools; it won't take me long to screw them together. The weight of the countertop will keep the island in place. What colour were you thinking?"

"Since the cabinets are natural wood, I was thinking espresso. The countertops are ivory, so a dark base should be nice. I just need to go to the paint store in town and pick some up. I need a few groceries as well, so I might be a while."

"Good choice, that should really make a statement in here. Take your time; I will keep an eye on the place while you're gone," said Gage now thinking he might have time to go back into the locked room. His only concern was running into Myles coming out of his room or going in, right now he was still in the garden painting and Finch probably wouldn't be home until later.

"Thanks Gage, is there anything you need while I'm out?"

Gage, thinking how to keep her out longer stated he could use a wide flat-head screwdriver and some paper yard bags. This way Raye would have an extra stop, the hardware store.

"See you later; I'm going to pick up some burgers for dinner too. How are you on the barbeque?" Raye chuckled.

"Even better than the stove," Gage replied watching Raye smile and nod as she walked away.

Chapter 6

Gage applied some oil to the door hinges, that's much better he thought as he quickly closed the door behind him. Making his way to the closet door he opened it, pulling on the chain to turn the light on. Taking a better look than before, he noticed her closet was quite large and deep compared to the one in his bedroom. Reaching into his right back pocket he pulled out two long thin pieces of metal leaving a very thin flat head screwdriver in his other back pocket in case he needed it. Placing the two metal pieces into the lock he maneuvered them. "Just a little more," he said to himself, "C'mon," and there it was, just like that the door was unlocked.

Gage reached in and took out stacks of money, an easy million he thought as he took them out looking over each stack carefully. What's this he wondered as he opened a small velvet draw string bag? It contained a beautiful necklace with rubies and emeralds surrounded by small diamonds.

"Gage, are you up here?" called Myles as he went into his room. "Raye's looking for you."

Gage put everything back into the safe and quietly locked it. He didn't want to have to explain to Myles what he was doing in Mrs. Willoughby's room if he got caught. He waited until he heard Myles shut his door and he came out closing the bedroom door behind him, locking it and quickly ran down the staircase to the kitchen to return the key hoping he didn't run into Raye. Now that he knew what was in the safe, he would wait for the right time. Heading to the kitchen he saw Raye standing in the doorway.

"You're back early; did you get everything you needed?" Gage asked hoping that she didn't notice the key was missing.

"Well, you wanting something at the hardware store saved me a trip to the paint store. I found what I needed there. It's beautiful espresso coloured furniture paint, something I hadn't even thought of. So, thank you again," Raye chuckled, happy with her choice. "What have you been up to?"

"I was in the upstairs bathroom putting a new washer in the tap, I didn't like the way it was shutting off and a little oil on the door hinges didn't hurt either," showing Raye the oil can and taking a screwdriver from his back pocket.

"Well, here are the wide flat-head screwdriver and the paper yard bags you asked for," stated Raye as she handed them to Gage. "I'm going to make some potato salad and a broccoli salad, and when I'm almost done making them, I will get you to take care of the barbeque."

"Sounds like a plan and thanks for getting these. Can I help in any other way before the barbeque goes on?" Gage tried to distract Raye so he could put the key back.

"You can get me some potatoes from the bin and peel them if you like, while I get the broccoli."

"Perfect," replied Gage. The potato bin was a large drawer inside a cabinet. On the side of the cabinet was a circular rod iron bar with hooks. Each hook was for each room. All hooks but one should be vacant. Gage quickly placed Mrs. Willoughby's key on the hook while Raye was getting the broccoli from the refrigerator. Then he took some potatoes over to the sink and started peeling them for Raye.

Raye looked over at Gage as she was preparing the broccoli salad. "It's nice to have someone helping me in the kitchen," commented Raye, watching Gage smile as he finished peeling the potatoes and placing them on the cutting board.

"Yes, it's always nice to have company, especially someone to share things with."

"You're right; I haven't had that since my parents passed. My ex-boyfriend didn't want to do anything together. He had his own interests, but to this day I don't know what his interests were besides other women."

"How long were you both together?" asked Gage, this admission piquing his interest.

"We were together six months. He was partly the reason I bought this. We met some time after the accident, and we planned to leave the city and buy this house. The money from my parent's home was more than enough to buy it. Steve was never interested in fixing anything or helping with meals. He even wanted to get married, but it was too soon for me. Then I found him in bed with the two women living here renting two of the rooms. He had his own priorities for sure and it wasn't me. The day that you came, you were right, I had been crying. That morning, I had kicked him out and his two lady friends."

"I'm sorry you had to go through that with everything else you have been dealing with," Gage said, shaking his head as he placed the potatoes in a pot of boiling water.

"Thanks, Gage, I appreciate it. What about you, is there a lady in your life? Although you haven't left here since you came, so I'm guessing probably not at the moment." said Raye, convinced he was in-between relationships.

"You would be right; it's actually hard to find a genuine, down-to-earth person, someone that is compatible with you, someone that wants to be in a relationship with you not just in a relationship all about them. So, it's been a while. I think I just gave up. Sometimes your own company is good enough . . . for now."

"I agree, I am just glad I didn't marry Steve. By the way, while I was at the hardware store I bought a new lock for the front door. Maybe if you have time tomorrow you could change the lock for me. Steve still has a key to the front door, and I really don't want to ask for it back."

"Absolutely, I will do it tomorrow," Gage said as he drained the potatoes then rinsed them in cold water. "Here you go Raye, is it time to start the barbeque?"

"Yes, and the hamburgers are in the freezer. One for me will be fine, maybe two each for you and the others." Gage nodded as he went outside to start the barbeque. Thinking of Raye in another man's arms was starting to annoy him. She deserves a lot better than that Steve guy for sure. Gage wasn't sure why he was upset. He wouldn't be staying too much longer anyway, and he had had enough of failed relationships himself.

It was almost six and Myles was already outside talking to Gage. Finch had just come through the kitchen doorway, just in time to help Raye carry the salads outside to the patio table. One more trip to get the tray filled with the condiments, paper plates, cutlery and lemonade, then they could sit down to eat.

Raye set the table then took a moment and glanced over at Gage. His cargo shorts fit him snuggly in all the right places. Raye wondered why she hadn't noticed it before as she watched his left bicep bulge as he flipped the burgers. His dark-brown hair and facial scruff was becoming attractive as well to Raye. Gage must have felt Raye's eyes on him as he looked over to see her. She dropped her head quickly, not wanting him to see her staring at him.

"Come and eat," Gage said as he walked to the table with the hamburgers. Myles and Finch were having a discussion of their own and ended it knowing the food was on the table.

"This looks and smells wonderful," Finch commented as he reached for a bun taking his time to indulge.

"And it tastes good too, Myles stated as he took another bite of his burger. The salads are really delicious. You two make a great couple . . . I mean when it comes to cooking." Raye and Gage looked over at Myles smiling, now trying to get out of what he said so as not to embarrass anyone.

"How was your day Finch, is the university as good as you thought?" asked Raye.

"I think it is going to be even better. I know I'm going to like it here. I already met a few people that will be in some of my classes and the town is just as nice as my home in Fir Falls. I brought my camera, so I'll be able to take pictures of birds in the area. Maybe I will do a paper on one of them. I was wondering, would it be all right to put up a few bird houses, Raye? They just might have families move in.”

“I think that will be a great addition to the backyard. What do you think Myles? Would you be able to paint pictures of birds?”

“If they sit still long enough,” Myles chuckled, “if not I would do it from memory or maybe Finch’s photos.”

With the others in conversation Gage heard a car pull into the driveway and got up to see who it was. After Raye telling him about Steve, he didn’t want any uninvited visitors. He looked over the gate and saw it was Parker, home at a decent time, wondering if he would be joining them.

Parker had talked to Steve earlier and Steve wanted to try a trial run of him getting into the house and staying the night in Parker’s room. Parker came through the front door not knowing where anyone was. He had Steve in the car hiding in the back seat, waiting for Parker to give him the all clear.

“Get out of my way, stupid cat,” Parker said, taking a swing of his foot to Sidney, unable to make a connection although scaring him and making him run in the opposite direction. Parker could hear laughter coming from the kitchen. The French doors were open, and he could see them all sitting around the table on the patio, enjoying each others company. Good he thought, as he turned around and went to the front door waving Steve in.

Steve closed the car door quietly and made his way in. Parker had given him the key to his bedroom, but Steve needed to try his house key to the front door thinking Raye had changed the lock. It still worked, he thought, now thinking he could enter any time after eleven when the door was locked.

"I'll meet you upstairs, I should say hello, so it doesn't look suspicious. I have to keep up appearances," said Parker brushing his hair back off his brow as he left Steve and walked to the kitchen. He just wanted this whole thing to hurry up and go away.

Parker stood in the doorway watching the pathetic morons he terribly disliked as they were having a nice time. "Hi Parker, would you like to join us?" asked Raye, as she noticed Parker standing there. The others stopped their conversation long enough to say hi to Parker, not really wanting him to stay and ruin their night.

Parker wasn't really interested in small talk and didn't want to get to know any of them. He wanted to help Steve out and move on, sooner the better. "Thanks, I already ate and I am a little tired. I'm going to turn in early, I just wanted to say hello and let you know I was home. Good night, everyone."

Each one said good night, and then carried on with their conversation, as Parker left the patio. "What a bunch of jerks," Parker said under his breath, shaking his head as he made his way upstairs to his room. Lowlifes, he thought, yeah that's what they are, grinning as he entered the bedroom doorway.

"What are you grinning about?" asked Steve, as Parker closed the door.

"Oh nothing, I was just thinking about the lonely-hearts club going on outside. Who needs people like that?"

"Yeah, don't let it bother you. As soon as I get some money we'll be out of here. You just keep up the facade and I will take care of everything from here on in. Give me a week and this should be over."

Parker nodded his head liking the sound of that, plus the fact that it was all in Steve's hands now. "So, what's the plan?"

"I figure when everyone is out of the house, I will go into the old woman's room and open the safe. One night I cozied up to her with a few shots of bourbon and I found out she can't hold her drink. She told me she was buying a safe and asked me if I would bolt it to the floor for her when it was delivered. I'm not sure how much money she has, but after selling the house to Raye, she must have hundreds of thousands . . . maybe even a million. I just need to pick the lock and open it up. When I lived here, I had a key to her room made, so it won't be a problem getting in."

"Sounds like you have thought of everything, dear brother," said Parker lying on the bed ready to close his eyes. "I have another big day tomorrow—night."

Steve knew the rest was up to him as Parker was never any help. Steve could tell Parker what to do and he would follow directions, but he could never think for himself. Maybe that was a good thing Steve thought, as he watched Parker sleeping. "We've come a long way little brother and the money in that safe will set us free. Just a few more days and we can leave this crappy, out of the way, no mans land, kind of town. "Just a few more days," Steve whispered aloud, quietly letting the world know their journey was almost over.

Steve took the extra pillow and put it on the floor below the window, just like old times he thought when he was in foster care waiting for a family to rescue him and Parker. They never came and they both grew up in the system waiting for a second chance. Lying on his back he crossed his ankles, placing his hands behind his head on the pillow, dreaming of the money that would change their lives. "Tomorrow is one day closer to the wealth that is owed to us, little brother . . . one day closer."

Chapter 7

"Raye . . . Raye," called out Finch as he half ran through the house carrying a box, looking for her. He spotted her outside watering the planters that adorned the patio.

"There you are," he said placing the box on the patio table, his mouth grinning from ear to ear.

"What's going on Finch, you're so excited?" asked Raye smiling as she sat the watering can down on the slate patio stones.

"The bird houses, they arrived, and I can't wait to show you. They are the same ones I have at home and a few others I couldn't resist," said Finch, eagerly opening the box and lining up the houses on the patio table.

"What's going on?" asked Myles standing in the doorway hearing all the commotion Finch was making.

"Look Myles, they arrived, the bird houses I was telling you about. Aren't the colours exquisite? They're all hand made and beautifully hand painted, something I think you can relate to Myles."

"It is an art for sure and you're right, Fresher, beautifully executed." Raye smiled and looked at Myles realizing he had given Finch a nickname, reflecting how he sees him, being a freshman at university. "Where's Gage, he should see these beauties too?" said Myles.

"He's in the basement, hooking up a sink so he'll have somewhere to wash up after his yard work. He didn't want to use the upstairs bathroom or the main floor bathroom."

"You certainly picked a good handyman Raye, he never stands around idle, always doing something."

"You're right Myles, he is always busy. First thing this morning he put a new lock on the front door for me, which I had been meaning to change. But it was really Gage who found me and I'm very fortunate for sure." Raye took her eyes off of Myles and looked around to see where Finch had gone. "He's so quick, where did he go? Finch!"

"I'm up here, I just need to go up a little further," Finch said as he stepped up on a higher branch of the huge sycamore tree. "What do you think?" he called down to Raye and Myles now standing at the bottom of the tree. "Just one more loop and it will be secured," said Finch as he tightened the rope on the bird house around a small branch.

"C'mon down, Finch," called out Raye, worried that Finch was too high up.

"I'm coming," said Finch as he turned to put his foot on another branch and missed it all together. Down he came trying to grab onto the branches as he fell to the ground.

"Are you all right?" said Raye looking at Finch lying on the ground.

"It sure looks great up there; the birds are going to love it for sure."

"Oh Fresher, never mind the bird house, are you okay?" Myles shaking his head wondering if Finch was all right. "Get up, let's see."

"Yeah—yeah, I think so." Finch, taking help from Myles tried to stand up. "My left ankle hurts, I can't stand on it."

"You're lucky that's all that hurts. I knew it, I just knew it," said Raye. "No more tree climbing for you. Use a ladder next time or get Gage to put them up for you. You'll have to go to the hospital and get that looked at."

Gage, distracted by all the commotion outside, left the installation of the sink to see what was going on. By the time he got outside he saw Finch sitting on a patio chair with his foot up on another chair. "What happened?" he said, looking at the three of them puzzled.

"Fresher here fell out of that huge tree trying to hang up his birdhouse," offered Myles with an explanation.

Gage stood there shaking his head and grinning. "You're young, it will heal but an x-ray is probably in order."

"Could you help Finch to my car Gage, and I'll take him to the hospital. We might be a while so on the way back I'll stop and pick something up for dinner, any suggestions."

"Hmm . . . what about chicken?" suggested Myles, not giving the others a turn in deciding their dinner. Raye looked at the other two waiting for a response and just smiled. "Okay then, chicken it is."

Gage and Myles helped Finch to Raye's car putting him comfortably in the back seat with his leg up on the seat as well, Finch now looking as though he was in agonizing pain. "A stiff upper lip, now Fresher," said Myles hoping he would be okay.

"Thanks boys, see you soon." As Raye pulled out of the driveway and down the road, she looked at Finch in the back seat through the rear-view mirror. "Don't worry

Finch I'm sure they will give you some meds for the pain."

While Raye and Finch were on their way to the hospital Gage and Myles decided to put up the rest of the bird houses. They might not have been as high up as the one Finch put up, but definitely high enough above ground to avoid any animals disturbing the families that were to move in. The one nice thing about the bird houses that Finch bought was the size of the hole in every house. Each one was for a different bird species which would make for enjoyable bird watching.

"Thanks Myles, Finch will be glad this is done. I have an hour before the men come with Raye's countertops. With all the excitement, I bet she forgot they'll be coming today. Oh well, it'll be a surprise for her when she gets home."

"Can I give you a hand Gage; it might be easier with two of us?"

"Yes, it would be, thank you, Myles. Just let me get the tools and I'll see you inside."

Gage and Myles worked well together. Gage unscrewed the countertops from the cabinets and both men used a pry bar to lift the countertops up. Once they were loose, they carried them out and put them at the back of the driveway. The men coming with the new countertops agreed to take the old ones and recycle them. Gage and Myles threw the last one on top of the other two. It was the smallest one that was used as a desk area in the kitchen.

Gage looked up as the truck with the countertops had pulled into the driveway. "Nothing like timing," said Myles looking at Gage checking his watch.

"They are a little early, maybe thinking we would run into a problem taking them apart," Gage said looking at Myles. "We're all ready for you!" he yelled over to the men. "It will be easier for you to bring them in the back way, right into the kitchen."

"Thanks man," said the taller of the two men opening the door to the back of the truck. Myles followed them as they carried a countertop into the kitchen with Gage leading the way. Everything went like clockwork as they installed them all. The only thing left was to install the new white farmhouse sink that Raye had purchased. The men had brought it with them as it was part of the order plus six chairs for the island. The sink had to be flush-mounted and the front piece of the cabinet had to be cut in order to accommodate the sink. These men could have done it with their eyes closed, thought Gage. They knew their job and did it well, even Myles was impressed.

"Thanks again guys, nice job. The lady of the house will love it," said Gage as they finished loading the old countertops into the truck. Off they went and Gage went back into the kitchen, wondering how much longer Raye would be. Myles was wiping the counters down for Raye. Neither of the men wanted her to have to do anything when she got home.

"What do you say we eat at the island tonight? Myles asked. "We can set up the dishes and take the wrapping off the new chairs, this way she can see it all set up when she gets home."

"Great idea Myles, and this colour she picked out for the island cabinets looks great with the countertop. She is really going to be pleased . . . yep, really pleased."

Gage went down to the basement to finish what he started, and Myles carried on getting the kitchen ready for Raye. He went outside to get some cut flowers for the kitchen and did a once over on the kitchen floor. Everything was ready so Myles went outside to do some sketches for some new paintings.

"You can make it Finch, just one more step," said Raye as she opened the front door. "You'll soon be a pro using the crutches."

"Yeah, easy for you to say," laughed Finch, high on medication.

"Let's go to the kitchen Finch, I'm sure the others are hungry, and a little food wouldn't hurt you either."

Making their way to the kitchen, Raye stopped dead in her tracks while Finch was tottering over to the kitchen table. She had forgotten the countertops were coming today. The kitchen looked beautiful, and everything was exactly like she had pictured in her mind. What a wonderful surprise, she thought as she turned around to see Gage and Myles standing there smiling. "Thank you, guys; you did a lot of work today. This will always be so special to me, thank you so much . . . let's eat!"

The three of them sat at the island while Finch sat at the table with his foot on a chair. They listened to Finch as he told them of his ordeal at the hospital. The good news was that it was only a bad sprain. "It could have been a lot worse," said Myles and he let Finch know that both he and Gage had put up the rest of the bird houses. All he would have to do is enjoy the families that move into them.

"Thanks guys, I appreciate it," said Finch as Raye took him a plate of chicken with macaroni and potato salad. "And thank you Raye for taking me to the hospital and for this great dinner."

"You're welcome, Finch, we all have a lot to be thankful for," said Raye smiling at Gage and Myles.

"You really picked out great countertops Raye, said Gage as he helped himself to more potato salad. The espresso paint colour with the countertop on the island really stands out. Nice job!"

"Thanks Gage," replied Raye just as Gage's cell phone rang with the ringtone being a country song. He excused himself and went out on the patio to answer it.

"Hey, it's been a while. Yeah, I opened it . . . a million and a jeweled necklace. Yep, I can meet you tonight. Same spot, say around nine. Okay, see you then." Gage made his way back into the kitchen. "Sorry everyone, not often I get a call."

"That's all right, I'm just going to dish out the pie, would you like a slice?" asked Raye.

Gage nodded his head then gave an affirmative, "yes please."

Everyone else had already put their order in. "Did you guys make yourselves lunch while Finch and I were gone? I left tuna salad in the refrigerator for sandwiches."

"Oh blimey, well luv, Gage and I got so busy we forgot about lunch. But we made up for it tonight. Not to worry, there is always tomorrow for tuna sandwiches," said Myles as he sat back in the chair taking a deep breath.

Finch swallowing his last piece of pie dropped his fork on his plate. "I just remembered I have a meeting with The National Audubon Society from seven to nine o'clock tonight. I don't suppose anyone would be willing to drive me there?"

"I will Fresher, I wouldn't mind seeing what all this bird stuff is about, but first the dishes and then we'll go."

"No, no," said Raye, "I'll take care of the dishes. I would like to use my new farmhouse sink, you two go and enjoy." Gage looked over at Raye letting her know he was going out too. "Well, I guess I will have the house to myself until Parker comes home," said Raye wrinkling her brow not really happy being alone with Parker. Her face became more relaxed as Gage told her that he had come home around four and left again, basically in and out. All she needed to do was enjoy her night.

With the guys gone the house was quiet. Raye stood by the patio doors looking at her new kitchen. It was stunning with the new countertops and the island complete. Raye smiled as she visualized her mom and dad sitting at the island. *Pass me some sugar Anna. Oh, Eddie, you know you don't take sugar. Just from you Anna, just from you.* Then Anna would laugh and give Eddie a kiss . . . how Raye missed hearing their cute flirting and how much they really loved each other. Their affection for one another was intoxicating and it gave Raye a feeling of comfort, being in a love filled home.

Her dad would sometimes put on some music as her mom was cooking dinner. In-between stirring the pot, he would grab her for a dance or two around the island and back to the stove again. He was always doing things on the spur of the moment which brightened up their day, especially mom's day, he loved her so much. He was a happy-go-lucky kind of guy and was liked by so many.

When Raye was little, and no one would play with her at school he told her to sing a special song in her head and the kids would come and play with her. To this day she still wasn't sure how he knew they would come and play with her. Singing his song didn't make her feel lonely, she always felt like she was on top of the world and nothing else mattered. A smart man he was, as she sat there picturing him talking to her. The memories were starting to come back to Raye, flowing generously through her mind. Was she finely coming to terms with their death? "I hope someday I find what you both found together . . . I miss and love you both very much."

Chapter 8

Gage left after Myles and Finch. He told Raye to enjoy her alone time and that he would be back late. She smiled thinking he really did have a life other than what he had there. Maybe some day he would tell her all about it she thought but tonight was hers and she had plans to organize the kitchen.

Gage pulled out and headed to the highway as it would take some time to get to Hamden Shore. It was a city south of Turnersfield known for its boat shows and fishing derbies. It took him over an hour to get there and another half hour to get to the docks. Gage pulled in behind a large boat house and turned off the lights and the motor to his car. He grabbed a flashlight as he closed the car door. He flashed the light over to an old boarded up garage that had a few broken windows on its second storey. He knocked on the door and someone from the inside opened the door. The garage smelled of old fish and oil combined. Not the most pleasant of places to go into Gage thought, as he entered the building.

"Good to see you," said a man with a deep voice. "Were you followed?"

"No, too many on-ramps . . . the painting in her room is a real Monet. I'm sure there are more valuable paintings throughout the house as well as artifacts. There're a lot more people living in the house now, I need to be careful."

"Let me know about the other paintings. I'll take care of everything else at my end."

"Will do," said Gage. "Oh, and here."

"Right," said the man, taking the envelope Gage handed him.

Gage nodded and left the garage. The conversation was over and all he could think about was getting back. Walking back to his car he got in and pulled out of the parking lot as he thought of Raye having an evening to herself. It wasn't like him to think of others as he only had to rely on himself and what he wanted. Was he beginning to have feelings for Raye or was he enjoying being a part of something more than just himself? What was she doing? Gage wondered as he drove from Hamden Shore on the northbound lane, home. Home, he thought, it had a nice ring to it, but he was there for a reason and the money was only part of it. At the moment all he could think about was Raye and wondering what she was doing.

Since she had more cupboard space in the island Raye decided to add things from her over stocked pantry. She had moved a lot of small appliances to the cupboards below. This would be easier when she needed them. She looked up from what she was doing and saw Sidney coming through the doorway. "I wondered where you were, pretty boy. I left a piece of chicken for you Sidney, here you go." One sniff of the plate and the chicken was devoured. Sidney then licked his paw and started cleaning his face. A nap would soon be in order as he left the kitchen and headed to the den.

Raye stocked up the last cupboard with extra dishes she had stored in the pantry. They were her parents' wedding dishes that her mom had saved, wanting Raye to some day hand down to her family. Her mom would use them on special occasions then stack them neatly away until the next one. It was a tradition that Raye was hoping she would carry on, but for now they would sit undisturbed.

The house was quiet, which in the last little while had been anything but. She was actually glad to have some quiet time to herself, but she really did miss the guys. She wondered why Gage had to go out. It was the first time since he rented the room, and he said he didn't have a girl friend to speak of. So why now did he have to go out? she wondered. Why didn't he say where he was going? She had been honest with him, what was he hiding? Too many questions and no answers were beginning to frustrate her, something which was not worth pursuing. If he wanted her to know, eventually he would tell her and that was that. She had enough to deal with and carried on adding her little touches of décor to the kitchen. All the rooms in the house were cozy and beautiful but the kitchen was the heart of the home. It was Raye's favourite room in the house. It's where her family came together to cook, socialize and talk about the day's events.

Raye, getting tired decided to join Sidney in the den. As she entered the doorway she looked over at Sidney and smiled seeing him sprawled out in the windowsill sound asleep. Heading to the loveseat Raye picked up the remote control and turned on the TV as she sat down. The local news was on as she turned up the volume to hear the anchorman.

Raye turned off the TV thinking how Gage fit that description perfectly. No, she thought, he couldn't be, he's such a nice man. But then she thought Steve was too. Her mind was just racing at the prospect of Gage being a murderer. Just then she heard a noise coming from upstairs. It sounded like something had dropped on the floor or moved.

Raye nervously got up, quietly leaving the den and went into the dining room to retrieve the poker leaning against the fireplace. She clutched the poker as sweat ran down her palms. Raye held her breath as she slowly walked, listening for any more noises. The news of a murderer had upset her and thinking the man could be Gage was disturbing.

There it was again. She slowly put one foot in front of the other as she sneaked along the floor reaching the staircase. Slowly she went up one stair at a time with the poker in her right hand squeezing the handle tightly. Her heart was beating out of her chest and the anticipation of finding a stranger in the house was frightening. What if it was Steve getting back into the house, which was just as

70

worrisome. Maybe he came in when she was in the den; the front door was still unlocked until eleven. Raye reached the top of the stairs straining her ears, listening for any other noises. She noticed the light under Parker's door was on. All at once a thousand reasons entered her head why she should call the police and not try to apprehend an intruder herself or even confront someone. She was just unnerved at the prospects of someone jumping out at her as she leaned closer to Parker's door.

"Raye is everything all right?" said Parker coming up the stairs to his room. Raye's body jumped inside as she turned to see Parker. "You startled me Parker, how long have you been home? I thought I heard someone up here and I thought everyone was out."

"Yeah, that was me. I came up here and then went back to get something I forgot in my car. I didn't see anyone, so I just came to my room."

Raye looked at a paper bag he was carrying from the local burger joint. "Strange how you would forget a burger and fries in your car. The smell alone is a dead giveaway," said Raye now becoming a bit of a sleuth and feeling quite silly sneaking around the house carrying a poker.

"It's late and I'm tired. I couldn't eat it all so I figured I might eat it later," said Parker trying to distract her from thinking someone was in his room. If she found out it was Steve, the plan would be wrecked and for sure she would call the police on him this time.

As much as she didn't think much of Parker, his attitude had changed, and he deserved the benefit of the doubt. "If you would like some lemonade or fruit juice you can help yourself to some in the refrigerator."

"Thanks, Raye. I just might come back down and get some, good night."

"Good night," said Raye as Parker went to his room. She came down the staircase and headed to the dining room to return the poker, her body a little less stressed, actually relieved that it was Parker and not an intruder.

With the poker back in its place Raye saw Myles and Finch come through the front door. Raye smiled as they both looked happy talking about birds and what they do for nature and mankind. "This was a very informative meeting, Raye, about a lot of different bird species," said Myles looking at Raye as he came through the doorway and wanting to tell her all about his experience. "Fresher might be on to something. He told them I was a painter and might be painting portraits of birds. Some of them might be interested in buying some of my paintings. But more importantly they are all invested in the well being of birds."

Raye smiled at Myles. "Well, you just never know what one might find enjoyable. Good for you Myles for going, I can see Finch is glad you enjoyed it." Raye looked over at Finch, seeing he was very tired. "Do you need help upstairs Finch?"

"I've got this luv, we will see you in the morning," said Myles as he helped Finch to the staircase and up each stair one at a time.

Nice guys Raye thought, as her mind came back to the news broadcast, knowing she didn't have to worry about either of them being a murderer. Finch was too thin with the wrong hair colour, and Myles was way over the weight specifications. Parker didn't meet the height requirements, but Gage was still on her radar for sure.

He still wasn't home, and Raye didn't even know if he was coming home. Gage said he would be back late but maybe a special someone had changed his mind. What did it matter to her anyways? Raye thought. I really don't know anything about him. Was she becoming too dependant on him? He was just supposed to be the hired help. She needed to remember to rely on herself and not get involved. He never said he was staying or if he even liked it here. He made no commitments.

Raye's mind was working overtime, so she decided to take a shower and get ready for bed. The shower had put her in a more relaxed state, realizing that maybe she had overreacted to the noise. Raye turned off the water and opened the shower door taking a towel to wrap around her and a second towel to dry her hair. Next, she put on a silky pair of pajama shorts and a silky halter top. She then put on a robe, remembering she had to take out the garbage bag that she had left in the kitchen sink.

With the garbage bag in hand and the key to the small shed she put on her shoes and went out the front door. The outside light from the front door gave just enough light to see the passageway to the shed. The small shed was located within the driveway area and the door was always kept locked. Raye didn't want any animals or rodents getting into the garbage scattering it everywhere.

It was very dark out and the night sky was full of stars with a full moon shining down. The night air was brisk which was unusual for this time of year, but it felt refreshing she thought as she unlocked the shed door, opening it and adding the garbage bag to the blue bucket with a lid. Raye closed the shed door and locked it, then started walking back. "Oh no, where did it go?" Raye had dropped the key into the gravel in the driveway. That was another thing she had planned to get done in the coming years, but she wasn't sure what materials she wanted to do it in, as yet. Raye knelt down looking and feeling around for the key. This was almost like looking for a needle in a haystack, but not quite she thought, trying to see its reflection in the moonlight.

Raye looked up as a car pulled into the driveway, its lights glaring right at her. She froze like a deer in headlights looking into the night. The car door opened, and it was Gage with his flashlight in hand wondering what Raye was doing.

"Raye . . . Raye," he said trying to get a reaction from her, but nothing. He knelt down beside her with his arm around her waiting for her to acknowledge him or anything for that matter. She just kept staring in the direction of the car, frozen again in time. Then without warning she started crying, holding onto Gage tightly. She placed her head on his shoulder, all the while Gage letting her know he was there for her and that everything would be all right.

Raye looked up at Gage with tear filled eyes. "I saw the truck again Gage, I saw the door of the truck. I saw a "W" and a half circle. What do you think it means?"

"I don't know but I think we need to get you inside to bed and let your mind have a rest. C'mon, I'll help you up."

"I lost the key to the shed, somewhere here. I can't find it," blurted out Raye still kneeling on the ground.

"You mean this one," said Gage as he picked it out of the stones and handed it to Raye.

Raye smiled as Gage stood up, holding out his hand to help her up. Together they walked hand in hand through the front door, locking it behind them and down the hall to her bedroom. She placed the key on her bedside table then Gage helped her remove her robe. He helped her into bed, then covered her up and gave her a kiss on the forehead, all the while wondering if her fight from within would finally come to an end. "Sleep tight and we can talk more in the morning if you want."

Just then Sidney walked through the doorway and jumped up onto the bed. "You watch over her big guy," said Gage as he gave Sidney a patting on the head. Raye drifted off immediately, not even aware that Gage had left her room.

Gage went upstairs to his room, noticing all the lights were off in the rooms as no illumination was seen under their doors. It had been a long night for Gage and an unexpected one for sure. He kicked off his shoes and removed his gun from the waistband of his pants, placing it in the drawer next to his bed. Luckily his shirt had covered the back of his pants and the gun otherwise Raye might have seen it. He sure didn't want to have to tell her why he had it and what he was doing there. She was really beginning to trust him he thought, and didn't want anything to jeopardize that right now.

Gage removed his shirt and pants, placing them on the chair and opened the window. The curtains gently flowed as the night breeze entered the room, and the moon shone through his window as it danced amongst the clouds. He crawled into bed, placing a heavy head on his pillow, falling asleep instantly.

Chapter 9

"Come on Fresher, we have a lot of places to go this morning," said Myles as he tried to get Finch up and out of bed. "Come on!" he yelled knocking on his bedroom door.

"Okay, I'm up, I'll be down in ten minutes," said Finch as he grabbed his crutches and headed to the bathroom to wash up.

Myles all ready downstairs in the kitchen, sipping on a cup of coffee, said goodbye to Gage who had to pick up paint and supplies for the garden shed that Raye wanted fixed and painted. She wanted it to look like one of Finch's bird houses, very colourful and bright.

Finch closed the bathroom door and headed to the stairway as one crutch fell to the floor in front of Parker's doorway. Finch was glad that Parker left for work very early, so he didn't have to worry about waking him up and neither did Myles.

"Too bad I'm shut in here or I would give those two jerks a piece of my mind," Steve muttered under his breath as he heard the noises in the hallway. First Parker gets up and leaves, waking me up and now the two losers, yelling and banging on doors. Hopefully, they leave soon he thought, because today he was going to open the safe and get out of the house for good.

All seemed quiet as Steve gently opened his door and peaked down the stairway. He heard Myles in the foyer tell Finch that Gage had left to get paint to make the garden shed look like one of his bird houses. Finch thought that was a great idea and it would definitely make a statement for sure.

Myles and Finch left to get painting supplies at a craft store for Myles. He was going to paint a few portraits of birds for Finch to take to The National Audubon Society meetings.

"Finally," whispered Steve as he crept down the stairs and helped himself to a cup of coffee in the kitchen. But where was Raye? he thought, as he quietly went to what was once his bedroom, to see if she was there. He peaked through the doorway as she had left the door open just like he remembered. She hasn't changed a bit, just as he suspected, leaving the door open for the dumb cat. Seeing her in bed sleeping, he now reflected on how it felt having her body next to his.

"You'll wish you hadn't thrown me out. I'll have more money than you could ever imagine. We could have been a great couple together. You blew it bitch," Steve declared under his breath as he stared at Raye laying there asleep. "You're lucky you have people in this house that care about you, or I would make you wish you never threw me out."

Steve left the bedroom disgusted, heading to the kitchen to finish his coffee. Not wanting to run into Raye, he finished quickly and headed back upstairs into the bedroom to get the key he had to Mrs. Willoughby's room and the tools he needed to open the safe.

He placed the key into the lock and turned it slowly, opening the bedroom door. The room was full of light as he entered, closing the door behind him. She definitely had the nicest bedroom in the house and the view to the backyard was spectacular, which Steve checked to make sure there was no one back there. He checked the side windows that viewed the parking spots in the driveway. He noticed Raye getting into her car. "I wonder where she's headed, dumb broad," he scowled as he watched her leave.

Finally, Steve went to the closet and opened the door, pulling on the pull chain light to see the safe sitting in the back corner. "There you are, please be good to me," he whispered as he took two short pieces of metal out of the bag, placing them into the slot of the lock. He slowly moved the metal pieces back and forth waiting for the door to unlock. The sweat was starting to run off his face as he kept trying without success. "Stupid thing," he snarled, kicking the safe in anger.

He tried calming himself wanting to give it another try. Taking a deep breath, he moved the metal pieces back and forth again, this time in a slower motion. The door didn't want to unlock so he removed the metal pieces and tried using a screwdriver hoping it would work as he manipulated it, but still to no avail in opening the safe door. "Damn it," he moaned. If only I had taken that second key when it was delivered, he thought, now thinking the second key might be hidden in the room somewhere.

Steve took the screwdriver out of the lock and placed it along with the metal pieces back into the bag, then turning off the light he slammed the door behind him. He searched her dresser drawers in haste, not returning the drawers to their usual neatness. The drawers were left open with clothing sticking out. At this point Steve was anxious to find the key and didn't care how he left the room. He looked behind the painting, under the rug and even under the cushions on her chairs in the sitting area, throwing them to the floor. He knocked over tables in case she had taped it under one of them, but still no luck.

Steve pissed, took out his cell phone and called Parker. "Ya, it's me. I need you to pick me up. The plan didn't work; I can't get the safe open. I'll have to figure out a different way."

"Okay, I'll be there in ten."

Steve went out of Mrs. Willoughby's bedroom locking the door behind him. "You again, get lost before I kick you. Yeah, you better run, you scaredy-cat." Poor Sidney ran down the stairs looking for refuge. Steve laughed as he carried his tools back to Parker's

room grabbing his belongings and scurrying down the staircase and through the front door. He sat amongst the bushes in the flower bed waiting for Parker to arrive. There was a truck in the driveway parked along the side of the house. Raye's handyman must be home, Steve thought as he was beginning to panic that he might be spotted.

Gage had pulled up to the side of the yard to unload the paint and supplies he picked up from town taking them to the shed in the back yard.

Parker pulled up in the driveway quickly, the tires sliding in the stones as he braked. He saw Steve and unlocked his car doors for him to get in.

"The handyman's home, his truck's over there," stated Steve in a disturbed voice.

"Yeah, don't worry. He's probably busy in the backyard," Raye has him so busy he doesn't know if he's coming or going, poor stooge. Parker pulled out quickly leaving the place behind with Steve feeling a little more at ease.

The noise from Parker pulling up quickly on the stones was heard by Gage as he came up to his truck at the side of the house to get the paint. He noticed someone getting into a car the same colour and make as Parker's car. Strange he thought, maybe it was just someone that came to visit Raye and since she wasn't home, they would have to come back. He would be sure to let her know, but for now he needed to unload the truck as the weather was getting cloudy and it looked like it was going to rain.

Parker was already miles down the road as he listened to Steve about trying to find the extra key to the safe. Steve went on and on about how he could talk to a buddy of his and ask if he had anything he could cut the screws with, that were in the floor. Could he get a handsaw in between the bolts and the floor? he wondered. Worse scenario he could use a power saw and cut the floor around the safe and take the whole thing. He now had to think of all his options. Everyone would have to be out of the house if he used a power saw.

Parker dropped Steve at the house and really couldn't care less about Steve's options. It was his idea and up to him. Parker just wanted to wash his hands of the whole mess. He was happy to work a full day and party after hours.

"I have to get back to work. Let me know your plans," said Parker as Steve got out of the car. Steve nodded at Parker as he turned to walk away, not happy at today's turn of events. He was glad to be out of that tiny room and back at his house; a small rundown house that they rented. Next, he had to call a buddy or figure out himself how to get that safe open. He really didn't want anyone else to know because he feared they would want a share of what was inside.

"Hello . . . I'd like to know if you have a saw that can cut metal screws. That's great, a hacksaw or reciprocating saw. I'll be down tonight and buy both just incase one doesn't work. Thanks, bye." Steve, a little more confident called Parker to let him know that he was taking him to the hardware store after work. He needed to get this done before the old woman came home. He was surprised she wasn't home by now; she must be enjoying herself abroad. What if there wasn't any money in there? What if she spent it all? Steve realized he had no proof there was really anything valuable in the safe, only what she had told him. Maybe she was lying. Steve didn't want to think about that, he was willing to wait and see.

Parker was tired having finished a full day's work. He pulled into the driveway at the rooming house to get Steve's wallet. Steve had called him and told him it must have fallen out of his pocket when he was sleeping on the floor, maybe it was under the blanket he was sleeping on. Parker parked in his usual spot noticing everyone's vehicle was accounted for.

Entering the house, he could hear talking and laughing coming from the dining room. Parker couldn't be bothered to go and say hi to them. He didn't want them asking questions about where he was going. His life was his business, and he didn't like having people pry into it. Besides, Steve was waiting for him and the sooner the job got done the sooner he could leave this house and all the losers in it.

Parker opened his bedroom door and closed it, visually looking for the wallet on the floor. "Where is it?" Parker shook the blanket on the floor waiting for it to fall out. "It's not here," he said, shaking it again. This time he got down on his hands and knees and searched under the bed. "Nothing—where can it be?" he said, as he pulled the curtain back from the windowsill. "Oh, no, he must have dropped it outside in the flower bed." Hoping to find it Parker headed down the stairs and outside. The others didn't even know he had come and gone; they were all having a great time in conversation.

Parker looked under the bushes in the front flower bed and even under the hydrangea plants hoping to find it. He had to comb the brown mulch carefully that Gage had put on the flower beds last week. Being the same colour as Steve's wallet it was hard to see so he placed his hand down, running it over the mulch. "Nothing— Steve is going to be pissed."

Parker didn't want to be the bearer of bad news, but this time it wasn't his fault. Steve was becoming clumsy, not only in judgment but in his actions. Maybe it was time to walk away and forget his plan. No, he thought, Steve had helped him all his life, he couldn't leave him. It was sink or swim and if Steve could get the money they would be set for life.

Parker unlocked his car and checked the passenger seat just in case it had fallen between the seat and the console or even under the seat, nothing. As he got into the driver's seat and started the car, the clouds overhead looked a little dark and gloomy. He drove to the house;

rain drops hitting his car. Turning on his wipers, he called Steve to let him know he was on his way but didn't mention the wallet. Surprisingly, Steve never asked. He must have had too much on his mind. The rain had stopped, and the sun was coming out from in-between the clouds as Parker pulled up along the sidewalk out front, unlocking the doors so Steve could get in. "Well, where was it?" asked Steve.

"I didn't find it, it wasn't there." Parker could see the lid ready to blow.

"What do you mean? It has to be there!" Steve raised his arm and clenched his hand into a fist as his face turned red with anger. Abruptly he hit the dashboard of the car denting it.

"Stop, you need to calm down. I looked everywhere in the room, I even looked outside in the bushes thinking you might have dropped it. Maybe you left it somewhere else." Just then they both looked at each other. "It's in the old woman's room," they both concluded.

The drive to the hardware store was anything but pleasant for Parker. He had to use his card to buy the saws needed to cut the screws that bolted down the safe. The hacksaw would take longer but definitely less noise. The reciprocating saw would do the job a lot quicker for sure. The man at the store even sold Steve a pry bar which he said might be used to lift the safe up, prying the screws out of the floor, either way Steve wasn't taking any chances this time. He was going to carry that safe out of the house with part of the floor if need be. There where only two screws to cut and hopefully one of the saw blades or both would fit between the safe and floor.

Parker dropped Steve off hopefully in a better frame of mind. "Here take this key and go into the old woman's room and find my wallet, don't let me down." Steve slammed the car door and headed into the house.

Parker, tired of Steve and his belittling comments headed back to the rooming house. He was tired and frustrated at Steve's attitude making him feel inferior. It was all he could think about driving back. The streetlights were casting shadows as he turned the corner and headed down Terry Lane. He pulled into the driveway and parked his car. Long day he thought as he headed inside. The house was quiet and really, he couldn't care less where everyone was. All he could think of was having a good night sleep.

He climbed the staircase and opened his bedroom door. The bed looked inviting as he climbed onto it and sprawled out on his back with his arms over his head. He had a big day tomorrow as the construction company wanted him to take a crew to another job site.

This was his chance to show the boss that he had what it took to be a foreman. The men would have to listen to him which Steve would have been good at. Parker was the one that was always told what to do. He worked while Steve guided their life in the right direction. At least that's what Steve would say when he told him to get a job and pay for his share of the rent.

Parker could hear the others coming up the stairs and down the hall to their respective rooms, each one saying good night to the other. Parker sat up and pulled a bottle from his side table. A few drinks might help him get to sleep as he took a swig of whisky, then another, then another. The empty bottle lay on the floor as Parker snored the night away.

Morning came early as the others were up and having their coffee to start the day.

Parker still sleeping missed his wake-up call and most of the morning. His cell phone ringing numerous times was one of the guys from work calling to make sure he was on his way. "Hmm . . ." he said as he rolled over and stretched. "What a great sleep—oh, no!"

He got up and rushed down the stairs and into his car, hoping he could explain why he was late for work.

"What are you doing here?" Steve asked as Parker came through the front door. "No, never mind, you got into the booze again— didn't you? Do I always have to hold your hand?" Steve yelled as he punched the wall right beside Parker's face, putting a slight crack in the plaster. "I'm getting tired of your drinking and your stupidity. Did they fire you?"

"No, they need me. They suspended me a couple of days without pay and I lost the foreman job. Don't worry; I can still pay my share of the rent." Steve wasn't a labourer like Parker was. He used his brains to make his money or at least that's what Steve would tell him. He got paid monthly for taking care of websites for a few companies. Parker wasn't good with computers and only knew hard work, even his cell phone was used only for calls. Too many buttons he would say and when he pressed one making his phone inoperable, he would go to Steve to fix it.

"You let me know when no one is home, and I'll come in and take the safe. Keep your eyes open and no more drinking until this is over. Don't screw this up!"

Chapter 10

Days passed and Raye hadn't talked to Gage about that night in the driveway. After combing the house with a poker looking for intruders and thinking Gage might be a murderer Raye thought she was having a nervous breakdown. She needed to figure this out on her own and not get other people involved but she knew it was too late for that as they all knew she had emotional problems. Now she was going to stand up on her own going forward.

She had called the police in Bryerton to let them know what she thought she saw the night of the crash as the case was still open until they charged someone. Raye felt at peace with herself, like she had come full circle. Her brain had finally pieced the puzzle together. She needed to work on herself and find things that interested her.

Finch had asked her for a ride to the university this morning. He needed to go to the office and sort out a couple of his classes. His ankle was almost healed, but the doctor thought he should use the crutches for another week.

First things first she thought as she got dressed. Looking in the mirror she realized she could do a little more with her hair as it had grown a little longer. Maybe time to let it keep growing, she thought. Something to definitely think about as she had always had long hair growing up. A little blush on her cheeks and a little lipstick were the final touches of her makeup routine.

Raye put on a pretty dress with heels and made her way to the kitchen looking for Gage.

She spotted him outside painting the shed. It was a medium sized garden shed with a cedar shingle roof and shiplap exterior with decorative gingerbread trim. Gage and Raye had decided to paint it a bright yellow with white trim. "Good morning, Gage," said Raye as she stood there watching him paint. "I love the colour already, it's beautiful."

"It will stand out for sure, just like Finch's bird houses," replied Gage as he stopped painting long enough to look at Raye. "Good morning, Raye, you look very nice this morning."

"Thank you. I know you're busy, but would you mind making lunch for you and Myles today? I'm driving Finch to school. He needs to go to the office and see about his courses."

"Sure, I don't mind at all," replied Gage wondering why Raye has been a little distant lately. Is everything okay with you? We haven't talked about that night."

"It took me a few days to process but I'm fine . . . no I'm better than fine, Gage. My inner self is not fighting within anymore. I actually feel like a big burden has been lifted off of me and I thank you for being so patient with me and helping as much as you have. I did call the Bryerton Police Department and let them know what I saw, maybe it might help. I'm good though . . . really. I have to go, Finch is waiting." Raye smiled as she left his side eager to go to the university with Finch. In less than a month the university would be open to students, but the faculty members were already getting their rooms and courses ready, which Finch had mentioned.

This was a new beginning and a new day, a first of many Raye hoped going forward. Finch was already in her car waiting. It was a beautiful sunny day to be on campus and Raye could tell Finch was eager to get going. She smiled as she got in the car and buckled up. The university wasn't far from her house which is why Finch wanted to rent a room from her.

Approaching the university, the street was lined with huge trees and a walkway on either side leading to a beautiful building. Another road off to the right led to student parking at the back of the school. Raye had always seen the university from a distance, not really seeing it for what it actually was. It looked like a piece of history back in the day when castles were built out of stone. Now she was on her way to see it in all its glory.

Raye pulled into a spot right out front. It must be for faculty members she thought as only a few cars were there.

"Do you need any help getting out Finch?" Raye asked as she unbuckled her seat belt.

"No, I'm good, but thanks," said Finch eagerly wanting to get inside and get his classes straightened out. He had a backpack over one shoulder as he walked with his crutches putting a little weight on his almost healed ankle. The doctor told him, a little pressure on his foot would be good going forward.

The outside of the building was massive and powerful looking. It was truly a majestic stately old building, just like the castle Raye envisioned from a distance but even more grand than she had expected. Reaching the doorway Raye pulled on one of the door handles, then on the other. Both doors were locked as she rattled them hoping someone would come to open them, Finch looking at her in surprise.

A man with blonde hair and glasses leaned out of a window on the floor above the doorway. "You need to go to the side door to get in," he called to Raye and Finch. "The front doors are kept locked until school starts. I'll come down and meet you."

Raye and Finch made their way to the side entrance. Opening the side door, Raye and Finch stepped into a vestibule done in oak wainscoting and damask cream wallpaper just like the rooming house. From the vestibule ran a long hallway with a highly polished floor giving off a scent of being freshly waxed.

The blonde-haired man was coming down the hallway as Raye and Finch walked towards him. He was tall with large broad shoulders and wore black rimmed glasses. He looked like he was in his middle thirties. Although young he definitely looked the part of being a scholar, thought Raye as they approached him.

Now standing in front of them the man reached out to shake their hands. "My name is Tim Ashlee; I teach second year computer science."

"Nice to meet you sir, my name is Finch Edwards, and this is Raye Daniels, the lady I live with . . . no, I mean rent a room from."

The man wrinkled his brow as he looked over his glasses at Finch, and Raye gave a bit of a smirk. "I own a rooming house, and Finch is one of my guests. He came all the way from Fir Falls, Calgary to attend the Ornithology class."

"Have you now," said Mr. Ashlee, "it's quite the course and each year it's full, with other students wanting to get in. The professor is Mr. Weston and it's a very hands-on course as well. Expect to go on field trips young man. Only the dedicated and committed will pass and go forward, so don't take it lightly."

Finch nodded and thanked Mr. Ashlee for letting him know. Mr. Ashlee pointed Finch to the office that was two doors down on the right. "Miss Reynolds is in today," he added. "She's the one to see about any scheduling mishaps."

Raye watched as Finch left and she thanked Mr. Ashlee for helping them and being so nice. Before Raye could say goodbye to Mr. Ashlee a lady came up the hallway approaching them.

"Hi, Laura, how's your day going?" asked Mr. Ashlee.

A short middle-aged woman with dark-brown curly hair was fit to be tied. "I'm ready to pull my hair out."

"I know what you mean, this is rush time. Laura Stevens, I'd like you to meet Raye Daniels. She came with a friend so he could straighten out his courses."

"Nice to meet you, Miss Daniels. I love my job, and I don't like to complain but this year seems to have sneaked up on me. I have boxes and boxes to unpack, and I still have a few lessons to get ready. I had to wait for a few deliveries, and wouldn't you know they were late then they all came at once."

"I'd like to help you Laura but I'm at crunch time too," said Mr. Ashlee, sympathizing at her dilemma.

"I could help you, if you would like me too. I have to wait for my friend, and he said he would be a while," said Raye hoping she would be taken up on her offer.

"Well Laura, looks like you have a volunteer."

"It certainly does, and I would be happy to have you help me and thank you for offering. If we're going to be working together let us be on a first-name basis," said Laura now with a smile on her face, looking a little less stressed.

Raye thanked Mr. Ashlee again for being so kind then left him and went with Laura to help organize the room while she finished some of her lessons.

An hour had passed, and Raye had unpacked all the boxes and organized them on the shelves. "Thank you, Raye, you've been so helpful. Would you be interested coming here once a week to help me out?"

"I would love that Laura, would next Wednesday be all right, say nine o'clock."

"That's perfect Raye, I will see you then and thank you again."

Raye and Laura exchanged phone numbers before Raye left Laura's classroom, heading to find Finch at the office. She stepped into the office doorway and didn't see him. As she turned around to leave the office Mr. Ashlee passed by and asked her how she made out with Laura?

"I got all the boxes unpacked and I put all the books on the shelves. She was quite happy and wants me to come back next Wednesday. She is a very nice lady and very precise in what she wants so it will be a good relationship."

"Have you thought of taking any classes Raye?"

"Oh, I've gone through school all ready and have a nursing degree. I worked at the hospital in Bryerton in the Emergency Department. Then I decided to take a break for a while and moved here."

"Well, if there is anything I can help you with please don't hesitate to ask."

"Thank you, Mr. Ashlee, you have been very helpful."

"Please call me Tim and I will be seeing you again, I'm sure. Also, I saw Finch outside in front of the building. Enjoy the rest of your day, goodbye."

"Thank you again . . . goodbye, Tim," said Raye as she proceeded down the hallway to the side door. Walking around to the front of the building she saw Finch talking to a young girl his age, a cute young lady with a slim build and dirty blonde hair. She must be a freshman too Raye thought as she approached them. "Hello, I hope I wasn't too long Finch? Who's your friend?"

"Raye this is Megan, Megan this is Raye, the lady I rent a room from."

"Nice meeting you Raye. Finch and I have a lot of classes together."

"Yeah, if it wasn't for coming in today, we might not have become friends and it's always nice to know someone else in the class," said Finch looking a little flushed.

Raye could see Finch was impressed with Megan. "Do you live here Megan or are you from out of town like Finch?"

"My home is in Prince Edward Island," explained Megan. "It's a small town called Coots Ridge. Only a few thousand people, so everyone knows each other. It's like having an extended family."

At a young age I found a baby green-winged teal, a beautiful little duck that I named Charlotte. She would follow me everywhere and the more I read about her and how to help her, the more I wanted to read about the different species of birds I'd see in Coots Ridge. If it wasn't for finding Charlotte and raising her, I probably wouldn't be here today. She gave me the love I have for birds."

"That's a great story," said Finch looking at Megan with endearing eyes. "I'm so glad we met. Would you like to exchange phone numbers or maybe go out for lunch one day?"

"That would be great, Finch. I rent a room above the local diner so we can meet there and have lunch anytime."

"Perfect," said Finch while Raye smiled knowing these two would become very good friends. "I'll call you tomorrow, Megan," said Finch as he and Raye said their goodbyes.

The drive home was an interesting one. Not a word was said as Finch smiled all the way home. Raye glancing over occasionally could see the wheels turning as Finch was jotting notes on a piece of paper. Raye pulled into her driveway and parked her car. Finch put his notes in his backpack and hobbled out of the car. Raye got out careful not to disturb Finch's quiet mood. They both walked up the sidewalk to the front door; Finch stopped and looked at Raye.

"Thank you so much Raye," said Finch, breaking the silence, having an enormous grin on his face. "This was the most perfect day I have had in a long time and I'm so happy that you were a part of it and that I asked you to take me."

Raye gave Finch a hug and told him that she really liked Megan and that she would be helping a teacher on Wednesdays. So, he would be seeing her around campus from time to time. They both smiled at their eventful day as they walked through the front doorway, closing the door behind them.

Chapter 11

"Good morning, Gage, the shed looks beautiful. You've done an amazing job, it looks brand new," stated Raye, bringing a cup of coffee out to him thinking he needed a break.

Gage was just finishing a small flower bed on either side, adding the mulch. He had a few plants that needed to be divided in the other beds, so he made use of them.

"I can't thank you enough for all the work you have done. The place is looking new again and not so run down."

"It just needs to be taken care of like everything else," said Gage noticing how much happier Raye looked. Was there something he missed last night at dinner? She never talked about anything new. He decided to ask her. "You're very happy this morning, anything new?"

"Well, since you asked, I had a wonderful time with Finch yesterday. I met two teachers. One was Tim Ashlee and the other was Laura Stevens. I helped Laura unpack some boxes and she asked me to come once a week to help her out. I don't know for how long but it's going to be nice to talk to another woman. Oh . . . aw . . . don't get me wrong, I love talking to you, but women can relate to women, and I haven't had that in a long time. Also, Tim seems very nice too, he teaches computer science."

Gage laughed as she went on and on about her day. It was nice seeing her happy for a change, a constant happy. Was the real Raye coming out after being bottled up for so long? Gage sat back drinking his coffee amused at her facial expressions of Finch meeting a girl. Why didn't Finch mention it last night? he wondered, maybe he didn't want any razzing about the girl he met, answering his own question. Myles can also be intrusive at times, giving Finch the gears.

Her smile was becoming infectious as he just let her talk. Even the outfit she was wearing suited her. Her outfits were becoming a little more stylish and her hair seemed longer too as she had it pinned up on one side. Why hadn't he noticed this before?

"I think some ground cover at the front of the flower bed would be nice, what do you think Gage—Gage?"

He was indisposed, admiring her. She did have that certain quality about her, charisma and sex appeal all rolled into one. Woken up from his thoughts he agreed with getting some ground cover. "What about going now Raye, then I can finish the flower bed when we get back?"

"Perfect, I'll just get my purse and meet you out front."

Raye closed the front door and headed to her car. Not even thinking that he would drive, Gage honked his horn. Raye looked up and carried on to his truck as Gage got out and opened the passenger door for her. He held her hand as she stepped up onto the sidestep of his truck, helping her get in. Raye thanked him as he closed the door.

The drive to town was a pleasant one as Raye tried to find out more about Gage. "How long do you plan to be a handyman, Gage?" she asked, wanting to know how long he planned to stay.

"I'm just floating by the seat of my pants, right now. I take one day at a time and never look back. When I need to carry on, I will know when the time is right. You were kind to hire me and have made me feel welcome. I'm good for now."

Raye smiled at him and placed her hand on his, not even thinking. "I'm glad I hired you too. Stay as long as you like," she told Gage removing her hand and placing it in her lap.

Raye looked out the side window as Gage drove down the road. The roadway was lined with trees, nestled on beautiful, manicured lawns and the homes were just as impressive. Raye, taking her eyes off the scenery, looked over at Gage. What an unusual thing Raye thought as she saw Gage singing to music in his mind as his head went up and down with the beat. The radio was off, but he had a particular song in his head. Thinking back to when she was a kid her dad used to do the same thing when they went on a trip and her mom was napping in the passenger seat. Raye smiled thinking of such a nice memory. "Care to share, Gage?"

Gage, not aware that she knew what he was doing had to fess up and told her the song he was listening to in his head. "I knew it," Raye stated, "it was one of my dad's favourites."

"I think I would have liked your dad, Raye; he sounds like a great, thoughtful guy."

"He was, and he would have liked you too," she said with a tearful eye. "Now I have that song in my head and it's not going away anytime soon," she laughed, looking at Gage laughing too.

Gage pulled into the driveway of the nursery, picking a spot next to the carts. Gage got out and went to open Raye's door and took her hand to help her out. "I'll follow you with the cart and you pick out the ground cover you want."

Raye nodded and walked down the aisle of the nursery looking for the perennials. Gage was right behind her watching her every move. "What do you think of this one Gage, four on each side should give a nice start and maybe two each of these as well?"

"Great choice, I like them too," said Gage as he helped her put them on the cart.

"Oh, look Gage, they have a large pond and look at the baby geese over there, let's go and see. Come on . . . hurry," Raye called, as she was already over there looking at the baby geese, making sure as not to bother them as the mother was close by.

Raye bent down to put her hand in the pond watching the little fish pass by. Gage left the cart sitting as he wandered over to see her. Raye took some water and splashed it at Gage. "Slow poke," she laughed, splashing a little more at him.

"Oh yeah, my hands are bigger." He laughed, as he took a little water and splashed her.

They were going back and forth at each other laughing as the customers were standing there in awe, watching them. Their laughter was so contagious that they had some of the customers laughing with them.

Gage stopped splashing Raye and put his arms around her. He looked into her eyes and wanted to kiss her but remembered why he was with her in the first place. It was all he could do to restrain himself as she looked into his eyes. She pulled back realizing it wasn't the time or place to have a moment. She didn't want it to look like she was waiting for him to kiss her. If he had wanted to kiss her, he would have but didn't. Maybe a friend was all he wanted.

They went to the checkout so Raye could pay for the plants, not mentioning a thing about what just happened, then they headed to Gage's truck. He loaded the plants as he kicked himself for not giving Raye a kiss. He will never forget that moment, a moment he let go of. The ride home was quiet as the two of them had a lot to think about. Gage knew he had to say something to Raye so she wouldn't feel hurt or confused.

"Raye," he said taking hold of her hand. "About us back at the pond. I'm your hired help and didn't want to give you the wrong impression. I don't know how my life is going right now, and I like you very much and want to remain friends. I hope this hasn't hurt our friendship."

Raye looked at Gage with a half smile on her face. "It hasn't, I like you very much too and if it wasn't for you helping me through a bad time I wouldn't be where I am today. A very big burden has been lifted off my shoulders and you were a big help in making that happen. Never stop being you."

The stale air in the truck had finally subsided as Gage headed to the main street in town. "How about lunch on me at the diner, anything you want."

"I am a little hungry," said Raye knowing Gage was trying to make amends. "Oh no, I forgot about Myles and Finch, they'll be looking for lunch."

"They're big boys and can fend for themselves. They know where the refrigerator is." Gage pulled into the parking lot and turned off the truck. He got out and opened the door for Raye, helping her out.

It was a cute little diner with wooden floors and wood backed booths with red upholstered seats. The counter was made of stainless steel with bar stools in the same red as the booths. Choosing a booth near the window they both sat down. "This is the first time I've been here," said Raye, as she looked at the front of the menu that was already sitting on the table.

"I've been here once. The day I came into town to see if there were any rooms for rent in the paper and that's when I found you." Gage looked at Raye with a smile. "Well, what are you going to have? I think I'm going to have that big messy burger and fries," said Gage as he looked through the menu.

Raye opened hers and looked at the picture. It was one messy burger for sure with the works. "I think I will have the fish on a bun with coleslaw and a strawberry milkshake."

"Oh, a strawberry milkshake sounds good, why didn't I think of that? I'll have one as well."

"Can I take your order?"

"Yes," they both said as they looked up from their menus. Raye instantly recognized Megan. "How are you?" she asked, then introducing her to Gage. "I didn't know you worked here too."

"It made sense once I moved into the room upstairs and the cash will come in handy. I've taken quite a lot of hours for now but once school starts, I will have them cut back. I don't want my job competing with my study time."

Raye agreed with Megan that taking it slowly was the best thing to do as she knew firsthand what it was like to go to school and carry a job as well. As other customers were coming in Megan took their order and gave it to the kitchen to be prepared. "Nice girl, I hope Finch and her get together. I didn't want to bring up Finch as they just met. If it's right, it will happen."

"So now you're a wannabe match maker," Gage chuckled as he agreed she was a very nice levelheaded person that Finch would benefit knowing.

It didn't take long, and Megan brought their orders. Raye's eyes widened as she saw the messy burger and a third of the plate in fries that Megan put in front of Gage. "How are you going to eat that?" she blurted out as she looked at hers which seemed like a normal serving.

Gage looked at his plate ready to indulge. "Well, I could use a knife and fork but really there is only one way to do it and that's to pick it up and take a bite. What falls on the plate is up for grabs with the fork later." Without hesitance Gage picked it up and took a bite as his eyes anticipated the explosion on his palate from the pickles, onions, hot peppers and sauerkraut. "Wow . . ." he said, putting the burger down and picking up a fry. "Would you like to try a bite; I could cut you a piece . . . it's amazing?"

"No, it's okay, I'm happy with mine," said Raye as she took another bite and a sip of her shake. Today was a very nice day, she thought, her mind drifting as the conversation muted in-between eating. It was different from her usual days of staying at home. She really had no social life since Steve and anything they did they did alone.

She now saw through Gage that a partner should be more, even a friend should be more. He had a lot of good qualities even though she didn't know much about him. Why was he really here? she wondered, but maybe it didn't really matter as she, like Gage would now take one day at a time. Smiling, she watched as Gage took another bite of his messy burger, the juices trickling down his face. She picked up her napkin and reached over to wipe his chin. "One thing about a messy burger, they are just that," Raye giggled.

The drive home was pleasant as Gage pulled in and parked the truck along the side closest to the backyard. As usual he helped Raye from the truck and both of them carried the plants to the back. "It shouldn't take long to plant and water them," he figured, placing the plants he carried to the flower bed of mulch.

"You're right since I'm helping too. Where is the shovel, you can work on that side, and I'll work on this one?"

"Raye, that's what you pay me for, remember?"

Raye looked at him in a playful way, raising her eyebrows and tilting her head just a little, giving him a stern look. "I'm the boss remember, and if I want to help then I help and by-the-way thank you for a lovely day. . . so far," she laughed.

Gage, knowing when he was beaten gave her a hand shovel. They both laughed in conversation as they planted the flowers, definitely enjoying each others company. Even Myles, sitting nearby, could see how well they got along and how they complimented each other. He had that with his Louisa who he missed very much. Myles could see a difference in Raye from when he first came to stay. It was like someone, or something set her free. He walked over to the two of them as they continually flirted with each other.

"Is this a contest at who can do a better job?" Myles asked as he startled them.

"Hi, Myles," said Raye lifting her head . . . "no, we're just having fun. Would you like to help?"

"No luv, but thanks for thinking of me. You're both doing a great job. I have a painting to finish."

"A bird portrait for Finch?" asked Raye curious as to what he was doing.

"No, just one of my usual landscapes. I like to take my time and envision being there," he added.

Myles went to paint while Gage and Raye finished their planting. It didn't take long with both of them getting their hands dirty. Gage helped Raye up, both standing back to admire their work. "I'll water them Gage," said Raye as she turned to get the hose.

Gage stopped her in her tracks. "Nope, that's where I stop you. You like to play with water and I don't need a bath. Watering the flowerbeds is officially the handyman's job. It's been added to the list."

Raye burst out laughing looking at his face. "You're serious, aren't you? Okay, well I'll get us a glass of lemonade then I need to start dinner, we're having homemade lasagna."

While Raye was inside Gage watered the new plants as well as the others. The ones he previously planted were healthy and sturdy, doing well. Gage rolled up the hose thinking of Raye and how she was beginning to get under his skin. He had to go back into Mrs. Willoughby's room and open the safe. He needed to focus on why he was there. He shook his head as the temptation was becoming harder.

"Here you go," said Raye as she came up beside him.

"Thanks, it sure is getting hotter." Gage took the glass and put it up to his lips, taking a mouthful as Raye watched the sweat run down his face. Gage took the bottom of his shirt and wiped his brow exposing his six pack to Raye, something she had the pleasure of seeing before, during their encounter in the upstairs hallway. With their drinks in hand, they both went to sit on the patio where the wisteria vine over the arbour shaded them.

Myles was in his usual spot beside the fountain with an umbrella overhead. He said the trickling of the water was like calming music letting all the creativity flow to his hands.

Raye went into the house to make her lasagna while Gage went to take a look at Myles painting. "Where's Finch today, Myles?"

"He left before you and Raye got home. He's off bird watching. He wanted to take some pictures so I would have something to paint. I've never known anyone so fixated on birds. He's going to do well; I just know it."

"Yeah, I think so too," said Gage as he looked at Myles painting giving it the once over. "Your style is just like one of the old masters."

Myles looked at Gage in an inquisitive manner. "You know about different artists, Gage? You've been holding out on us all this time."

"Not really, we all took art classes through school. I just enjoyed reading on my own about different artists and their different techniques. Even the difference in their brush strokes I found fascinating and how they mixed their colours and what they used for paint."

"Which one?" asked Myles as Gage started to walk away.

"Hmm . . . Monet."

Chapter 12

"Laura at the university called and wants me to be there this morning to help her out. I should be back by dinner. I thought we'd have burgers and there is a salad in the refrigerator. Would you mind barbequing when I get home? Oh . . . and I'm afraid it's sandwiches again for lunch."

Gage smiled and told her not to worry he would look after the meals since he was not only a handyman but a cook too.

"Thanks Gage . . . gotta go!" Raye grabbed her purse and keys and left.

Gage couldn't believe he had the whole house to himself. Myles had an appointment in town to get his dentures fixed and Finch was going to the library to meet Megan. He was finally driving himself, giving his ankle a trial run and as for Parker, he went away on a week's vacation.

First things first he thought as he went to the kitchen to get the key to Mrs. Willoughby's room. "What the heck," he said as he searched the area. "It's always here, I know I put it back." Gage, now starting to wonder if Raye took it. No, she always leaves it here, he thought. I wonder if she knows it's gone or maybe she's been in the room and didn't put it back. I've wasted enough time; I'll just have to open it myself.

Gage went down to the workshop in the basement looking for Mr. Willoughby's Allen wrenches. He remembered seeing them in the drawer with washers and bolts. Finding them he took a thin one and another slightly larger. "This should do nicely," he said as he came up the basement stairs heading to the staircase.

Gage went to his bedroom to get the two long thin pieces of metal. "Sorry bud, I can't pet you now, here I'll leave the door open for you." Sidney went inside and jumped up on the chair near the window and curled up ready to have a nap.

Gage went to Mrs. Willoughby's room and stood in front of the door. He knelt down and put the thin Allen wrench into the lock. While pushing up and holding it in place he inserted the second one and pushed up on it and click, the door was unlocked.

Opening the door, Gage couldn't believe what he saw. The place looked like it had been ransacked. Someone had been looking for something and didn't care how they left the room. Gage noticed the painting on the wall was still there. He walked over to the closet and opened the door. He turned on the light to see the safe in the back corner. The safe was still there, thank goodness he thought. What's this? Gage bent down to pick up what looked like a wallet. He unfolded it and saw a drivers license inside; Steve Tealson 105 Waverly Road. Gage couldn't believe the would-be thief left his calling card. Raye's ex-boyfriend was definitely not a smart guy. Why wasn't his address the same as Raye's? Was he living two separate lives? Did Raye know? The questions were coming all at once in his head.

Gage put the wallet in his back pocket and knelt down pulling on the safe door. It was still locked. He took the two thin pieces of metal, inserting one at a time into the keyhole. Now it was just a matter of time. He maneuvered the pieces listening for a click and there it was. Gage took out the metal pieces and opened the door. "No! . . . it's gone, all that money gone and the bag with the jewels, gone too." Gage was fit to be tied as the million in cash had disappeared, where was it or better yet who took it? Was it still in the house or long gone? Gage needed to find that money. Was it Raye who took it or her ex-boyfriend Steve, maybe the two are in it together? Gage didn't see this coming. He locked the safe, turned off the light and closed the closet door. He left everything in the room the way he found it, locking the bedroom door behind him.

Puzzled and upset he went to his room, Sidney still curled up sleeping, enjoying the fresh air coming through the window. Gage sat on his bed looking at the wallet he pulled from his back pocket. "I didn't like him before and I sure as heck don't like him now," he muttered under his breath. "What did Raye ever see in a guy like that?"

That must have been Steve I saw being picked up out front that day, he thought as his mind was racing with numerous scenarios. He forgot to mention it to Raye and now glad he forgot especially if she orchestrated it. Then she would know he knew and who was it that picked him up?

There was still a chance that Gage could find the money; it could still be in the house but where? Gage took his cell phone from the night table and dialed a number. It rang a few times at the other end until the man with a deep voice answered. "Yeah?"

"Hey . . . the money's gone. Yeah, I know . . . it's not what we planned. It could still be in the house; I'll just have to search for it. I'll keep you posted." Gage hung up and left his phone sitting on the bed as he got up and paced the room.

Thinking of that day he saw Steve and the car that picked him up. He thought then that it looked like Parker's car. Could they be helping each other, are they friends? Parker could let Steve know when the coast was clear to get into the house. He will be back for his wallet for sure, Gage surmising the turn of events. All Gage could do now was check each room for the cash hoping it was still in the house. Was Steve successful in taking it, not realizing he left his wallet behind? But then what was he looking for in the room if he got the money? Maybe he couldn't open it and was looking for a key to the safe. But if he didn't get the money who did?

Gage would just have to wait it out and hopefully someone would lead him to the money. It wasn't over yet as all the paintings and artifacts in the house were still in place. They alone could be worth millions.

Gage upset, sat back down on the bed. Sidney, now awake wandered over to see Gage hoping to get a few pettings. Gage patted his head and stroked his back, while Sidney's motor was just a purring. "Well, Sid, what do you think? Too bad you can't tell me; you probably know a lot of what's going on around here." Sidney looked up and rubbed his chin on Gage's hand. "I better put these away, I might have a few more doors to open," said Gage looking at Sidney as he put his tools in the dresser drawer. "Come on Sid, let's go have lunch."

Sidney followed Gage to the kitchen and jumped up on one of the island chairs waiting for a bite to eat. Gage looked over at him as he opened the refrigerator and took out some ham and havarti cheese. Gage cut some ham and put it on a plate for Sidney, putting it on the floor next to his kibble. Sidney jumped down and rushed over to eat his treat. Gage made his sandwich and sat down at the island having taken out a soft drink as well. Not as good as a messy burger, he thought as he took a bite and smiled thinking about Raye and how she acted that day.

Sidney, happy with his lunch and the first one to finish was slapping something around the floor. From side to side, he played with it like he was playing hockey. At a standstill he was pawing it trying to get it out of the corner. "Sid, what are you playing with?" Gage smiling, watched Sidney, still hard at work trying to recover his toy, finally he got it free and slapped it over to the island. Gage looked down to see the elusive key lying on the floor as Sidney gave it another slap. "You scored!" called out Gage as he picked it up giving Sidney a pat on the head. "Good boy, you solved the mystery or at least one of them." Gage replaced the key to its proper place and finished eating his sandwich. Sidney, all tuckered out, went to the den to have a nap in the windowsill.

Gage washed his dishes then went to the basement to get a fixture for the upstairs hallway. Mr. Willoughby had a few sitting on a shelf and they had been accumulating dust not being used. Raye wanted the light changed for the vintage one in the basement. She felt it suited the house more and would give off more light since it contained two light bulb sockets. Gage took it off the shelf and cleaned it up using the sink he had installed. It certainly came in handy and worked perfectly.

First, he carried the light fixture upstairs placing it on the floor. Next, he went back to the basement to get the ladder and took it upstairs opening it up just under the ceiling fixture. Curious he tried Parker's bedroom door. It was locked then he moved on to Myles' room, it was also locked. Thinking Finch locked his as well he tried it anyway. The door was unlocked, which told him everything about Finch. He either had nothing to hide and didn't care if others snooped or that he thought people were honest like him and respected other people's privacy.

Gage entered the room opening the dresser drawers, looking through them neatly. Finding nothing he searched the closet next, just the usual clothes and empty suitcases. The desk drawers contained pens and pencils plus writing books for school. The top of the desk had his schoolbooks stacked ready for university. The only thing left were the bedside tables, "nothing," he muttered, then remembering to check under the bed, still nothing. Gage left Finch's room closing the door behind him still wondering if Steve had the money.

Gage climbed the ladder attempting to unscrew the light fixture on the ceiling. "Would you like some help?" said Myles watching Gage trying to juggle the light while unscrewing the screw.

"Sure Myles, if you wouldn't mind taking it," he said, handing Myles the fixture. "Would you mind passing me the other one but not the glass shade, that goes on last."

With the two of them helping each other the installation went quick. Gage stepped off the ladder and turned on the light switch. It was a beautiful light with a stained-glass shade, perfect for the upstairs hallway.

Raye was right, the fixture did give off more light and was well suited for the house. Myles carried the old light fixture to the basement while Gage carried the ladder. "Nice workshop," said Myles. "Everything you could imagine is in here. A mans paradise for sure if you're into fixing things."

"Yes, you're right; it's always nice to have the right tool for the job. How did your day go Myles? Did you get your dentures fixed?" asked Gage as he turned out the light above the workbench and headed to the stairs with Myles following him into the kitchen.

"They fit as good as new. They were getting a little loose and now they fit snug. He took awhile but he did a great job. Now these choppers are good on any piece of meat. Speaking of meat, do you know what Raye is planning for dinner and where is she?"

"She was called to go to the university and help out a teacher. So, she planned to have a barbeque with me cooking the burgers. She made a salad, it's in the refrigerator. Raye shouldn't be much longer," Gage said looking at his watch. "I guess I could get the onions and tomatoes cut up and ready to go. Finch should be coming through the door any second."

Myles helped Gage cut up the tomatoes and plate them, next was the onions. Gage's cell phone rang as he handed them to Myles. It was Raye calling, they had exchanged numbers the night he left to go to Hamden Shore. He knew he was going to be late and being by herself, he wanted her to feel safe. "Hi, everything ok?"

"Hi, Gage, yes, I'm good. Laura and I got a lot done today. She is such a nice person; I enjoy working with her. I won't be home for dinner, I've been invited out.

Since you were going to barbeque and there's a salad in the refrigerator, would you mind taking care of Myles and Finch?"

"No not at all, you should enjoy yourself. I'm glad Laura invited you out. I don't know her, but I like her already."

"Aw . . . no, it's not Laura I'm going out with, it's Tim. He asked me to join him for a bite to eat. Remember the computer science teacher I met? I shouldn't be too late, Gage."

Myles couldn't help but hear Gage's phone call. He could see Gage getting a little heated under the collar as his face was becoming a little flushed.

"Yes, I remember, we'll be fine here, enjoy yourself . . . bye."

"What are you crazy? I heard the whole thing. She's going to date another man. What about us?" said Myles as he teared up from cutting the onions.

"First of all, she is a grown woman and second we just rent a room from her, we have no say over what she does or wants to do," concluded Gage, trying to make it look like he was okay with her dating. I knew I should have kissed her that day, he thought maybe she would have thought twice about having dinner with that guy.

"Well, if she leaves us, it's your fault or if some guy moves in here and kicks us out, just saying." Myles took a seat at the island, pondering what it would be like without Raye. Myles just realized he had taken quite a liking to Raye. He thought of her like the daughter he never had.

Finch entering the kitchen heard Gage and Myles talking about Raye. "What's going on, has something happened to Raye?"

"No, she's fine, she just has a dinner date with a teacher at your school and Myles is upset."

"No . . . not Mr. Ashlee. He's a nice guy but likes pretty girls too. Megan was telling me things she heard from seniors that she met in the library. The gossip going around school is that he just dates and never makes a commitment and therefore goes from one girl to the next, definitely a ladies' man."

"Maybe he just hasn't met the right one, Fresher. Maybe that right one will be Raye!" Myles declared, still upset at Gage for not telling Raye how he feels. He could see it in their eyes that Raye and Gage were meant for each other. "I'm not hungry, maybe later. I'm going to my room." Off he went shaking his head. "Some people just can't see what's in front of them," he mumbled under his breath.

Gage was ready to eat. "Give me about fifteen minutes Finch and I'll have the burgers cooked. Meanwhile, there is a salad in the refrigerator if you want to get it out plus a couple of plates. I guess it's just you and me tonight."

It didn't take Gage long as he flipped the last burger and plated them ready to take inside.

"I thought you went to your room Myles," said Finch with Gage standing in the doorway with the cooked burgers.

"I changed my mind and thought I should give my teeth a test."

Finch and Gage looked at each other and smiled. "I have a couple here with your name on them Myles. . . let's eat."

Chapter 13

It was now well after midnight and Raye still wasn't home. Gage, with too much on his mind, wasn't ready for bed; everyone else had turned in early. Gage turned off the stove, taking the kettle and pouring himself a cup of instant coffee. He headed to the patio door and flicked on the outside light. She must be enjoying herself he thought as he sat in a lounge chair drinking his coffee. The night air was crisp and the sky clear of clouds. Every star in the universe was out, each one shining brighter than the next.

"I wonder what they're doing?" his mind totally fixated on this university, professor. He better be treating her right or I will have to pay him a visit. Thought after thought came into his head hoping she was okay. The night was so quiet and still even the crickets were silent. Gage, engulfed in silence heard a car door close and figured it was Raye as he checked his watch.

Raye humming Gage's country song came through the front door and locked it behind her. She did a little dance down the hallway and into the kitchen to get a drink of water. She was in a giddy state swaying from side to side. Raye noticed the patio light was on and saw Gage sitting there sipping a cup of coffee. He's up late, she thought as she opened the patio doors and went outside. "Hi, have you been waiting up for me?"

"Don't be silly, you're a grown woman. I couldn't sleep and it's such a beautiful night."

"You're right and the stars are amazing. Look, a falling star Gage," she pointed looking into the night's sky, "make a wish." Raye closed her eyes and made a wish opening them to see Gage looking at her. "Don't ask me, I can't tell you or it won't come true."

Gage smiled and asked her how her date went with the professor.

"If you mean Tim, it was good. We went to an Italian Restaurant in Hamden Shore and later we went dancing at this little pub down near the water. It was beautiful there; we saw the boats come in before dark. He's a nice guy committed to his work."

Gage took a sip of his coffee then tried to be social, "I'm glad you enjoyed yourself; everyone was asking where you were?"

"Aw, that's sweet and thank you for cooking the burgers. I might have to miss another dinner as Tim has asked me out again on Sunday. He's picking me up and we're going golfing. I've never been before; it should be interesting. He's going to show me how to hit a golf ball."

"I bet he is," muttered Gage under his breath, too faint for her to hear as he nodded at her and gave an "Uh-huh."

"Well, I'm going to bed. Thanks for always being there, Gage. I'm glad I can talk to you about anything, you're a good friend. Good night." Raye left and went inside to bed leaving Gage to dwell on his emotional issues.

Gage finished his last mouthful of coffee and went inside, placing his cup in the sink, washing it and placing it on the rack to dry. He turned the lights off and locked the patio door before heading to bed. Raye was home safe and sound and he could sleep knowing that. He passed Sidney coming down the staircase. "You know she's home now, don't you Sid," smiling at the cat realizing that everyone felt the same way as Sidney felt about Raye.

Gage opened his window, to the cool brisk air. His pants and shirt were placed on the chair as usual and into bed he went clearing his mind of today's events drifting into a deep sleep.

The house was quiet as everyone slept except for those out on the prowl. A car pulled up at the bottom of the driveway turning off its headlights so they wouldn't be seen. A figure of a man walked up the driveway carrying a duffle bag. Tripping over a rock the man fell trying to keep a painful cry from being heard. "Oh crap, that hurt," Steve muttered as he got up heading to the front door. Reaching the door, he took the key from his pocket and placed it in the lock. It would only go in halfway and no amount of pushing or wiggling it would make it work. She must have changed the lock he thought, now feeling angry.

Steve took out his cell phone and called Parker, waking him up to open the front door. *The person you are calling is not available. At the tone, please record your message or hang up now.* "Yeah, where the hell are you? This is the second time I've called and left a message. The first message I left I asked if you found my wallet and to let you know I was coming to the house tonight. Pick up, you moron!" Steve, royally pissed, hung up his phone and headed back to his car limping, thinking Parker probably fell asleep with a bottle in his hand. His car was in the driveway so he must be home in bed.

Steve drove away wishing he didn't have to rely on Parker. As long as the old woman wasn't back, I still have some time, he thought shaking his head at another unsuccessful try at getting the money.

Finally, back at his house he sprawled out on his bed too tired to look at the gash on his knee. It would have to wait until morning. Steve laid there in a sound sleep, not even hearing the birds outside his window singing loudly to welcome a brand-new day.

"Hey, Fresher, how about adding more water in the percolator? I have a feeling everyone is going to be up early and wanting coffee."

Finch looked up, seeing Myles standing in the doorway wearing his painting hat ready to start the day. "Good morning, Myles, why are you up so early?" Finch asked as he filled the percolator up to its max.

"I wanted to look at the pictures you took so I could get a start on painting a few bird portraits, the lights perfect this morning. I would like to finish a few before the meeting."

Finch taking out his phone showed Myles the pictures he took. He used a professional camera to take the pictures then he downloaded them from the camera to his laptop then to his phone. Now he could show Myles and even send him the pictures he would like Myles to paint. "This is one of my favourites," showing Myles the pictures. "This is a Chestnut-backed Chickadee with beautiful colours of black, white, grey and a rust-brown."

Myles looked at the pictures shaking his head smiling. "This one is just beautiful sitting on the branch with the greenery behind him and the light coming through hitting the leaves on the branch while highlighting the bird. The colours in all the pictures are so clear and bright. Are you sure you don't want to be a photographer instead, Fresher? These pictures are quite amazing; each subject is breath-taking. I will paint the five different birds to start then some of the different backgrounds of the same bird. That will give us a nice variety. I love this one in flight, before it landed, just beautiful! You certainly have an eye for photography."

"Thanks Myles, I guess photography could be a back-up if needed. Here you go," said Finch as he poured a coffee and handed it to Myles.

"Mmm . . . nothing like a fresh cup of coffee," said Myles as he sat at the island watching Finch send the bird pictures to his phone. "Perfect, I just might get two done today."

The smell of coffee was now throughout the kitchen as Gage stepped through the doorway. "Good morning, guys. Everyone sleep okay?" he asked as he grabbed his cup from the drying rack where he left it last night and poured himself a coffee.

"We're good, never mind that, did Raye get home all right last night? Did you wait up for her Gage?" Myles wanting to know all the details as Finch eagerly looked on waiting to hear all about it.

Gage sat down at the island tapping his foot on his chair, thinking about last night then answering Myles as he brushed his hand through his hair. "First, I didn't wait up for her and second, she had a nice time. If you want to know more, you will have to ask her."

Myles looked a little disturbed not getting his question answered in more detail and even Finch creased his brow looking at Gage in a perturbed manner. Gage, now feeling loathed spoke up in his defense. "Look guys, it's her business not mine."

"What's my business?" asked Raye as she entered the kitchen hearing Gage mentioning her. "Am I the discussion around a morning coffee?"

Gage, feeling the pull of being stuck in-between told Raye the guys wanted to know how her date went last night. "I simply told them they would have to ask you."

Raye looked over at Myles and Finch as they sat there waiting for any tidbit that she would throw their way. "Fella's I'm flattered that you care enough to want to know how things went. Just ask, if I want to tell you I will and if not then I won't." Raye turned to make herself a coffee instead of a tea this morning, leaving the boys staring at each other in dismay. Raye turned around to see their faces and laughed . . . "okay . . . okay, I had a great time. Mr. Ashlee or Tim is a very nice man."

Myles and Finch were now enjoying their coffee, while getting the news firsthand from Raye. Gage sat listening, not really eager to hear it all over again. If he got up now it would seem rude to Raye and the others, so he made himself another coffee to distract himself.

Raye started from the beginning when Tim took her in his car to a restaurant in Hamden Shore, leaving her car at the school. Gage lifted his head not knowing this, thinking she drove herself to the restaurant, all the while being in his car seated next to him.

"The restaurant was beautiful inside and had a very cozy atmosphere. He ordered surf and turf and a bottle of wine. While waiting for our meal we talked about our interests. The evening was going really well until our meal came. We both removed the lobster tail from the shell. They came out pretty easy except there was a small piece of mine still in the shell. I tried to get it out with my fork, prying it and prying it until it came out and whipped across to Tim's plate. The look on his face was one of pure shock. I was so embarrassed all I could do was laugh."

"Oh, no, what did he do?" asked Finch attentively listening to Raye as were the other two.

"Well after the shock wore off, he laughed too. I was just glad it didn't land in the bowl of warm garlic butter, which would have been messy. After the delicious meal he took me dancing at a pub in the harbour. After a few dances we went outside and watched some boats come into shore. Then he drove me back to get my car and I drove home. That's pretty much it."

There was one question that Myles was waiting to ask. He knew it would bother Gage but only if he cared for Raye. "Did he kiss you goodnight?"

Raye turned her back to make another coffee, smiling to herself. Gage abruptly said he had things to do and left the kitchen. Myles and Finch were waiting for an answer. "We all care about you luv," stated Myles, "including Gage."

Raye looked at them both and smiled. "No, I didn't get a kiss goodnight. It's far too soon for that."

"It sounded like you had a perfect night, are you seeing him again?" Myles, still on a roll, trying to find out as much as he could.

"Yes, on Sunday. He's taking me golfing; it should be quite interesting since I have never golfed before."

"It's pretty easy, all you do is hit a ball and make sure you wear a good pair of running shoes because you'll be doing a lot of walking. We're all glad you had a good time Raye," said Myles as he got up and gave Raye a hug. "I'm going upstairs to get a canvas and my paints then outside before the good light goes away. Fresher has a few pictures to show you."

Finch had another coffee with Raye showing her the bird pictures on his phone. "They're beautiful pictures Finch. Your photography is outstanding. Maybe this is your calling."

"Thanks, Raye. If it is, time will tell." Finch smiled feeling quite happy with himself. He couldn't wait to see the paintings once Myles was finished.

"Excuse me, Finch." that sounds like the door knocker. Raye went to answer the front door. A large, tall man with greying hair dressed in a dark suit stood on the other side. "Hello, can I help you?"

"Are you Raye Daniels?" he asked while carrying a folder under his left arm.

"Yes, can I ask what this is about?"

"I'm a detective with the Bryerton police department. May I come in Miss Daniels?" he said, showing Raye his credentials.

"Oh, of course, please come in," said Raye becoming confused as to why he was here in the first place.

"I'm Detective Brady, Will Brady. You called our office in Bryerton about the car crash and the death of your parents. You told us about a logo you might have seen during that night. I have brought a few logos on paper and thought you might be able to identify the one you saw. Now you stated it was a "W" with a half circle."

"Yes, please come and sit down," Raye escorting him to the kitchen. "Can I get you a coffee, Detective Brady?"

"That would be very nice, thank you."

Finch had gone outside to tell Gage, thinking he might want to hear what's going on. Gage and Finch came through the patio doors as Raye was looking over the logos. Raye lifted her head and introduced the guys to Detective Brady then continued to look them over. Gage could hear her quivering voice and stepped over beside her. Standing next to her at the island he grasped her trembling hand letting her know he was there for her. With her tense body a little more at ease now, she looked the logos over. There was only one that was comparable to her visual flashback. "This one," she stated loudly, pointing to the last one. "This one for sure."

Detective Brady circled the one Raye picked out and thanked her for her resilience in this on-going matter. She certainly deserved to have an ending so she could move on and he was going to try to give her that.

Gage escorted him to the front door thanking him for coming. Back in the kitchen Finch was letting Raye know that everything would be okay. Raye looked at Gage entering the kitchen, nodding her head. "I'm good . . . it's just another step and hopefully my mind's eye is correct."

Myles came into the kitchen carrying his art supplies looking at their facial expressions, "What did I miss?" he asked.

Raye smiled as Gage and Finch went outside not wanting to fill Myles in. "Well, Myles . . ."

Chapter 14

Morning came quickly, especially for Parker as he got up at dawn. "Coffee's on," Parker told his buddy as he watched him slowly making his way to the kitchen, holding on to his head.

"Wow, we must have started drinking early. I don't even remember going to bed."

"Yeah," laughed Parker. "The last thing I remember was us taking turns downing shots. But I don't remember what the count was; I guess we'll have to do it again tonight."

The morning air was cool with the sun just getting up itself. The birds were singing in speculation of a beautiful day while the rest of the forest creatures were cautious of intruders in their home. "Joe, I'm just going to clean my rifle, then I'll be ready to go. It won't take me long."

"Yeah . . . yeah, take as long as you want, it's going to be a slow day," stated Joe just as happy to go back to bed. "I might need a few more coffees so I can see straight. I wouldn't want to shoot anything that's not legal to shoot," he laughed thinking about the raccoon he shot yesterday, just for the fun of it.

Parker took his rifle and cleaning kit to the table and sat down taking his cell phone from his back pocket. He had a notification that there were two messages. Not too concerned thinking it was work he put his phone on the table and took out a rod, patches and solvent from his cleaning kit. Parker took pride on how clean he kept his rifle, being the only prize possession he had.

It didn't take him long and he was ready to go but Joe had a different idea. He had gone back to bed leaving Parker to either go on his own or find something else to do. There was a boat down at the dock if he wanted to go fishing but Parker wasn't much of a fisherman. The only thing he really loved to do was drink. The more he drank the happier he was because the drinking drowned out Steve and his voice that was always in Parker's head.

The cabins were old and built out of what looked like barn board. The land surrounding the cabin was filled with large trees and shrubs extending all the way down to the water. Parker stood on the front porch and looked over at the next cabin. A car had pulled up and two girls got out grabbing their bags and headed inside. Maybe they could use a hand Parker thought as he wandered over knocking on the door.

"Good morning, ladies, I'm at the cabin next door and I saw you pull up. Can I be of any help?" Parker stood there leaning with his one arm raised and stretched out with his open hand on the door frame.

Both girls came to the door and saw Parker standing there in an obviously rehearsed pose. The blonde girl rolled her eyes as the brunette girl came forward and stood right in the doorway pointing her finger. "We came to get away from men like you and have a peaceful vacation. Now bugger off and don't come back. We're not interested in what you're selling."

That was definitely not the welcome Parker was expecting. "I'm sorry I asked, bitches. You're just two dumb broads that can't even get a guy. Watch your backs," scowled Parker as he walked away fuming at being put down like that.

Parker went back to his cabin slamming the door behind him. He put on his hunting vest and hat then he made sure he had lots of bullets. Joe was still sleeping and wouldn't know where he was, so he took his cell phone and slipped it into his back pocket. Next, he picked up his gun and left the cabin with vengeance in his eyes but not before grabbing a bottle of bourbon to bring along.

He took the trail that headed upstream away from the populated area. This looks like a spot we tried yesterday he thought. Having no luck there, Parker went on further. The morning was becoming quite hot as Parker took off his vest and shirt allowing his skin to be exposed to the elements. He hung them on a low tree branch as he headed deeper into the bush. Finding a spot, he hid among the bushes that contained a large tree at its base, waiting for a deer to pass by. It was early and he had the whole day to wait and hopefully Joe would join him. Parker sat with his back against the tree indulging in a swig or two of bourbon. He slowly put the bottle down as he saw a deer coming his way. He picked up his rifle and aimed, getting the deer in his sights. Just one squeeze of the trigger and he had his kill for the day. Just as he was taking the shot his cell phone started ringing. The unusual ringtone was so loud that it scared the birds that had nestled in the tree branches above. The deer bolted and disappeared into the woods to live another day.

"Yeah?" said Parker putting down his gun and taking another swig of bourbon.

"Parker, why haven't you been answering your phone? I left two messages, why haven't you got back to me?" Steve yelled, taking all of his frustrations out on Parker.

Parker now oblivious to any messages because of the bourbon sinking in laughed at Steve. "I don't know what you're talking about. I'm on vacation."

Steve paced the floor even more upset. "What do you mean you're on vacation? The two days you had off are over."

"Because they gave me two days, I asked for the rest of the week off using vacation time. A buddy of mine asked me to go hunting. I work hard and thought I deserve some time off to do what I want to do."

"Did you get my wallet before you left?" asked Steve, hoping Parker found it.

Parker, getting a little irritated at being questioned about his every move, told Steve to leave him alone or he wasn't coming home and he could run his little scheme alone. Parker paused and took another drink trying to remember the question. Taking a second, he responded, "No, I didn't have time and if it's there it's not going anywhere." Parker slurring his words kept the conversation going. "I will look for it when I get back if no one's around."

Steve, shaking his head, knew it was no use talking to him anymore. The booze was kicking in and Parker was out to lunch. "Okay little brother, enjoy your vacation. I'll see you when you get home." Steve hung up and threw his phone against the wall shattering it into pieces. "What a piece of garbage," he fumed, realizing Parker was useless. Not only was nothing going according to plan he now needed a new cell phone.

Steve envisioned Parker lying in the woods drunker than a skunk by now as he wondered what his next plan would be. He needed Parker more than ever and would have to cater to him to get what he wanted out of him. Steve a little calmer left the apartment to get a new cell phone.

Parker, just as upset as Steve took another mouthful, almost finishing the bottle. Parker picked up his phone that was lying on the ground ringing, thinking it was Steve again having second thoughts. He would just tell him what was on his mind and get it over with.

"Yeah, Steve, you listen to me . . . what . . . oh, Joe . . . yeah buddy, I'm at the same spot as yesterday, I think. Yeah . . . I'm wasted, bye." Parker hung up dropping his phone beside him as he sprawled out over the ground.

Joe and Parker, having been friends for years would get together twice a year and go hunting. Joe knew that drinking and hunting didn't go hand in hand and needed to find Parker before dark or before a bear did. Joe knew enough to leave the drinking back at the cabin.

Joe, a tall broad heavyset man put on his vest and hat, taking a backpack as well filled with water, bear spray, food and a thermos of coffee. He also put his ammo belt on, not taking any chances knowing hunters always needed to be prepared. He didn't see this coming when he got up this morning, now wishing he had stayed up instead of going back to bed.

It was midday and still no Parker. Joe checked all their usual spots but with a year's growth of vegetation even their hideouts didn't look the same. Joe stood still as he heard something coming through the brush, placing his hand on his rifle. He quickly stood behind a tree watching as a mother deer and her baby passed by looking for food. Some of the bushes were covered in berries just ripe enough to eat. "Not now mama, we'll meet again," he said as he headed further up stream to look for Parker.

Joe, really feeling the heat took off his vest and shirt, then put his vest back on. If there were other hunters out there at least he would be highly visible in his orange safety vest.

"Gotcha," Joe said as he slapped a mosquito on his arm. The majority of mosquitoes were dormant as the sun beaded down on the dry foliage surrounding his every footstep.

"Parker!" he yelled hoping Parker would hear him; nothing but a few birds answered back. Joe took out his phone hoping Parker would answer it, but again nothing, it went to voice mail. "Where are you buddy?" Joe asked out loud hoping he would find Parker soon. One thing Joe knew for certain was that Parker was still in range, since his phone went to voice mail but not close enough to hear the ringtone. If Parker had gone deeper into the woods and higher up in elevation his phone would have no service.

Joe pressed on hoping he was going in the same direction Parker took. He was looking for any signs of an orange vest. "Where have you gotten to?" he asked under his breath as he looked ahead carrying on his search.

The wind was picking up and the sun had gone behind some clouds giving the woods an eerie facade.

Shadows of the stately trees were more pronounced as they manifested their grandeur over the landscape below. Up ahead Joe sighted a glimpse of orange through the leaves as the trees swayed in the wind moving everything in its path. It was Parker's vest and shirt hanging on a tree branch. At least he knew he was on the right trail but where Parker was now was anyone's guess.

The sky was becoming very dark; definitely a storm brewing thought Joe. He needed to find Parker now if they were to get back in time before the storm hit. Joe took his phone from his pocket and called Parker, hoping he was now close enough to hear the ringtone since he found his shirt and vest. The leaves were rustling as the wind was picking up speed racing through the trees.

Joe could hear them in the distance getting louder and louder as he proceeded quickly. Thank goodness Parker's ringtone was dogs barking and howling in the night. It made him feel safe and chose it because it reminded him of the night when he was five and Steve chased the monsters away under his bed at the government home. Scared, Steve barked and barked saying he would rip them to pieces if they didn't leave. From that night on Parker slept soundly not having to worry about monsters under his bed.

Joe never thought the sound of barking dogs would be music to his ears. He ran over to a tree surrounded by bushes and there was Parker lying face down in the dirt. "Parker are you okay, buddy?" said Joe as he rolled him over. Parker didn't make a sound as Joe propped his head up putting Parker's shirt and vest under it. Joe reached into his backpack and pulled out the thermos of coffee. Lightly slapping Parker on each side of his face he finally got a response from Parker, opening his eyes.

"What . . . what . . . stop," said Parker trying to focus on who was in front of him.

Joe opened the thermos taking off the cup and the screw cap then pouring some coffee into the cup. "Buddy, it's Joe . . . here, have a sip of this."

Parker took a sip of coffee, another and another as Joe sat beside him. "Finish it up so we can leave and get back to the cabin." As soon as the cup was empty Joe filled it up again. Parker needed to be somewhat sober if Joe was going to get him back.

An hour went by as Joe sat with Parker talking to him and reassuring him everything would be okay. It was probably good that the weather was getting bad; the dangerous wildlife would be hiding from the coming storm instead of looking for food or them in their path. Joe would be surprised if Parker would remember anything from today's events in the woods.

Parker, finishing the last of the coffee handed the cup to Joe. He then stood up and staggered over to a nearby tree to relieve himself in the shrubs. Joe packed the thermos away and handed Parker his shirt and vest to put on. He picked up Parker's phone and handed it to Parker to put in his pocket. He placed Parker's gun into his backpack on the opposite side of his with the barrel sticking up.

"It's time to go Parker, fellow me and be careful where you step, watch where you're going," stated Joe as he placed one arm through a shoulder strap of his backpack, swinging the pack onto his back then placing his other arm through the other strap. Finally securing the hip belt he was ready to go. Parker didn't even think why he was there or why Joe was there; he just followed him.

The wind had picked up even more and the sky was getting darker. The two of them moved quicker as lightning illuminated the sky with each step they took. As Joe and Parker ran quicker a wind gust blew their hats off. Joe was able to grab his the second the wind took it but Parker's was long gone. Parker was keeping up with Joe, running in long strides as the booze was wearing off, his cardio working overtime.

"We're almost there!" yelled Joe as a big crack of thunder stopped them dead in their tracks and rain fell drenching everything in its path. Joe and Parker took shelter under a tree huddling together, waiting for the rain to let up just a bit so they could see where they were going. A good fifteen minutes had gone by then suddenly a break in the rain.

"Ready!" yelled Joe as they both started running, seeing the cabin in their sights. They both ran towards it not looking at what they had left behind. Reaching the cabin Joe opened the door; then closed it behind them, finally safe from the storm outside.

Chapter 15

"Myles, these are beautiful, has Finch seen them yet? The colours are amazing and so true to life," commented Raye looking over the three paintings sitting on the patio, drying.

Myles was finishing up on another one, getting them ready for The National Audubon Society meeting tonight. Finch said they were eager to see some of the paintings.

"Thanks, luv, I'm really enjoying this, it's not my usual thing but it's nice to do something different. Finch hasn't seen them yet; he went to see Megan rather early this morning. I think he has a love interest. Yep . . . he's smitten for sure." Myles nodding his head as he added another brush stroke to his final painting. "The money for the paintings goes towards my paint supplies then the rest to The National Audubon Society. I'm not sure what to charge; maybe I'll wait and see what they're willing to pay."

"Sounds like a plan, Myles. It's nice that you use your talents for a good cause. Finch just adores you; I can tell."

Myles smiled and nodded. "I like him too; he's a nice kind-hearted kid. There . . . now I just need to sign my name and another one done."

Raye and Myles looked over as they heard the side gate open. Gage was carrying a bag of cement to fix a few minor cracks on the fountain and to repair an ornamental bird bath he found in the shed. "You look

135

awfully hot, can I get you a glass of lemonade, Gage?" Raye asked.

"That would be great, thanks. I thought you would have been gone by now." Gage, remembering she had a date to go golfing. While he waited, he took off his shirt and wiped his brow exposing his fit body to the sun.

Raye handed Gage the cold drink, then watched him drink some as the water droplets forming on the glass rolled off hitting his bare chest. "Thanks, Raye, that was very refreshing; it's just what I needed." Raye smiled, not sure if she even wanted to go golfing, now. The scenery had just gotten interesting.

"Hello . . . hello," said a voice coming from the side of the house into the backyard.

"Tim," called out Raye going over to greet him. "I'm sorry I lost track of time and didn't know you were here."

"That's okay, I knocked on the front door and when no one answered I heard voices back here, so I figured you were here," Tim explained, smiling at Raye eager to meet the others.

Gage was checking out his rival; not really what he had pictured in his head but definitely a scholarly looking fellow. Gage reached out his hand as Raye introduced him and Myles did the same. There wasn't time for small talk as Tim said they should be going. Gage figured he wanted as much time with Raye as he could get, showing her how to hit a golf ball.

Tim and Raye walked to his car. He immediately opened the door for her. "You look very nice," he stated as she got in, then closing the door behind her. Raye smiled and thanked him; glad she had put on her pink sweater and white shorts. Tim was taking Raye to a golf course on the outskirts of town. It was the only course around other than going to the one in Hamden Shore. Since Raye was a novice, the course they were going to would do just fine; it was a nine-hole golf course.

Tim pulled in and parked close to the doorway. He opened Raye's door and escorted her inside and over to the counter to rent some clubs for her. "I can just use one of yours Tim I don't need a whole set."

Tim looked at her with a raised brow, thinking it over. "No, I think you having your own will be good, besides they will be a lighter weight than mine; they're specially made for women. Which ones do you want Raye?"

Raye looking them over decided on the pink set as they matched her pink sweater. Tim paid for the club rental and the use of a cart as well. Already to play, he drove the two of them to the first hole. There was a group of people a few holes ahead which Tim was thankful for and no one behind them as yet. He knew it would take Raye a little while to catch on.

Tim took out his club and placed a tee in the ground placing a golf ball on it, showing Raye how to stand and swing to hit the ball. His ball sailed through the air and landed on the green. There were trees and bushes to the left and right of the fairway, which he said would be best if she stayed away from. The idea of the game was to get the ball in the hole in the least number of strokes he told her.

Now was Raye's turn, as she grabbed the club he suggested she use. She tried standing in a similar pose looking at Tim for guidance. He placed her feet in the right position and stood behind her with his arms around her showing her how to hold the club. Then he went through a practice swing with her. They tried it a few times before he put a tee in front of her and a ball on top, then stood away from her. Raye looked over at Tim and smiled then she took a swing and connected with the ball hitting it hard, sailing it into the air.

"It's not a bad shot for a beginner, at least distance wise; it just landed in the bushes," Tim announced as Raye laughed thinking she did pretty good.

Tim drove them down to get their balls. Tim's was on the green and Raye's was nowhere to be found. Not sticking with the rules, he told her to look for hers while he carried on hitting his ball. Raye's turn should have been next, but he wanted to get his over with because he felt she was going to take too long. In a stroke and a putt his ball was in the hole. Raye was still looking for hers. "Have you found it?" he called, walking over to where she was.

"Nope, do you think a squirrel took off with it?" she said jokingly.

Tim smiled and told her she could hit another ball close to the bush since she couldn't find hers. "There you go, now hit it towards the flagstick." Tim explained to Raye that every hole had a flagstick in it, showing the golfers where the hole was.

Raye, feeling confident, put a tee into the ground placing her ball on top. She took her stance with Tim watching her and nodding his head, then he corrected her hands on the club. Raye remembered to take a few practice swings. She looked towards the flagstick then the ball, then the flagstick again and then the ball. Raising her arms up she took a hard swing, hitting the ball. It popped up into the air and went backwards down into the bushes, losing her ball again. "Oh, no," she cried, "not again!"

It took her eight strokes to get her ball onto the green with Tim helping her with the putting, finally getting it into the hole. The next five holes pretty much went the same way. Tim was looking a little miffed as it was getting close to lunch. The people ahead of them were long gone and anyone that was waiting to play the hole they were on; Tim would give them the wave to play through. No one was put out because of Raye's playing, except maybe Tim.

Three holes to go and the water hole was next. Raye spent more time looking for her golf balls than she did talking to Tim. Now Raye's turn, she again took her stance and swung hitting the ball off the tee. It was actually a good swing thought Tim; she just needed it to go straight down the fairway onto the green. Instead, it was a line drive right into the water.

Raye knew the procedure. Being such a nice day instead of waiting for Tim, Raye took her club and an extra ball to the water waiting to place the ball on the outskirts of the water hole as Tim was finishing up. The sun was so hot, and the water looked refreshing. Raye sat at the pond's edge on a large rock thinking of taking off her socks and shoes so she could dangle her feet in the water while waiting for Tim to join her with the cart. Raye couldn't help thinking of Gage and how they would be splashing each other by now and laughing. Tim was only concerned about finishing his game.

Rayed noticed Tim wasn't going to bring the cart anytime soon, as he carried on with his game and was already at the flagstick, probably waiting for her. "Why invite someone to play golf if you're not going to play with that person?" Raye muttered as she swung her club, finally hitting the ball in the right direction. Tim was beginning to look like a bad date, Raye thought, so very inconsiderate.

The last two holes were better for Raye as her swing and hitting strength were improving; each time they landed on the far end of the green. Tim was actually showing a sense of humour and had lightened up a bit.

Finally finished they headed back to the club house. It was packed with people eating and having a few drinks while waiting to play. As they entered inside the people stood and applauded Raye. "It only took you seven holes to straighten out your swing, well done," said a man sitting at the counter. "I was rooting for you." Raye and Tim looked at each other and laughed along with everyone else.

Hungry, they sat down at the counter and ordered some food while enjoying the company of others. Tim was talking to a woman beside him who had passed him a piece of paper and Raye was talking to the man that was rooting for her and his wife who was sitting beside him.

It was three o'clock and Tim had another engagement or so he said. Raye figured it didn't go the way he figured and someone not being able to golf was a negative in his book. After they went into the club house, he pretty much talked to the woman next to him, laughing the whole time. Not a polite thing to do in her book either or leaving her at the water hole to finish while he carried on.

Tim, wanting to leave, rushed them from the club house to his car; opening the door and closing it before she was all the way in. For most of the drive home there was silence with a few in-betweens about how he was going to be late for his other appointment. Funny how the woman beside him left the same time they did, thought Raye shaking her head at the games people play, another Steve for sure. Tim headed down Raye's street and into her driveway. Everyone's car was parked, including Parker's in his usual spot away from everyone else's. He had a buddy pick him up when he went on vacation but now his car was backed in signaling to Raye that he had used his car today and was home now.

Tim pulled up in front of her house, not even getting out of the car to open her door. Raye got the message and said thank you for a great experience and goodbye, thinking he probably had another date after he dropped her off. "I'll see you at school Raye, when you come in to help Laura. You'll be a great golfer some day, keep practicing." And that was it, easy come and easy go, painless actually, Raye thought as she smiled realizing he was just a guy testing the waters for a good fit. Maybe he will have better luck with the girl at the clubhouse.

Ray entered the house hearing Finch and Myles having a discussion about the paintings. Finch was meeting with a few of the members for dinner before the meeting and wanted Myles to come too. He wanted Myles to show his paintings at dinner and Myles wanted to wait until he showed everyone together at the meeting. Raye was the deciding vote. Finch agreed with Myles and Raye to save the unveiling for the meeting. Finch helped Myles put the paintings into his car and then they were off to meet the others.

Raye took off her shoes and headed to the kitchen to start dinner for Gage. She wanted to cook something special for him as he was always helping her out. Plus, she was just in the mood to cook. She couldn't believe she had spent just about the whole day with Tim. It was almost four-thirty, a little early to eat but she wanted to make chicken parmesan and spaghetti. It would take her a while to prepare plus she wanted to simmer the sauce as well.

Raye went to the refrigerator to get a pepper, an onion, one stalk of celery and a clove of garlic. Closing the refrigerator, she noticed the basement door was ajar and the light was on. Gage must be in the workshop she thought and called down to let him know she was home.

"I'll be right up," he called out as she placed the vegetables on the cutting board.

She went to the cupboard above the stove and took out a bottle of red wine that she had purchased last week, just for times like this. It certainly hadn't been a very good date, and she was a little sore, so the wine should relax her. The best part of her day was sitting at the water's edge. I guess the standing ovation came in second she thought, smiling as she envisioned the crowd clapping. Amazing how one girl could stop everyone from playing golf. Raye opened the bottle and poured herself a drink. "Mmm . . . just what I needed."

Gage turned off the basement light and closed the door, looking at Raye and wondering how her date was. "Hi, do you want some help?" he asked, hoping she would let him know how it went.

"Sure, if you would like to dice this pepper for me, that would be great."

Gage took out another cutting board as Raye poured another glass of wine and sat it in front of him. He cut the pepper on its side, horizontally. "Damn it," he winced grabbing a paper towel.

Raye went over to see what he did. "It doesn't look bad, come and sit down." Raye took a clean towel and wrapped it around his hand and told him to hold it tightly while she went to get the first aid kit. Raye pulled up a chair in front of him and cleaned the cut with alcohol then added some antibiotic ointment to the gauze pad placing it on the cut. She took his other hand and placed it on the gauze pad and told him to put pressure on it while she got a roll of gauze from the kit along with some tape.

"Here, you deserve a sip of wine for being such a good patient." Raye placed the glass to his lips as he took a sip looking into her eyes. "You can take your hand off now," she stated, handing him the glass to hold. She wrapped the gauze around his hand tightly securing the wound, next taping it so the gauze would stay wrapped.

"There you go, almost as good as new," she said gazing into his eyes. Gage wasn't going to miss another moment with Raye. He stood up and pulled her into his arms, placing his lips on hers giving her a long sensual kiss. Raye's breath was taken away as he held her tight not wanting to let her go. She didn't resist which told Gage she felt the same way.

"Dinner will be late," she stated as she led him into her bedroom. This time she closed the door, not letting even Sidney into the room.

Chapter 16

"Good afternoon, Sidney," said Myles as he came up the staircase and headed to his room. Sidney was in the hallway trying to get into Gage's room. "He's still in the kitchen, come on, you can come in my room, come on," said Myles tapping the side of his leg coaxing Sidney into his room as he opened the door. "Here you go; you can have the box my paints came in." If it was anything that Sidney liked was curling up in a cardboard box which Myles found out numerous times.

Myles was working on a painting before lunch and wanted to get it finished. Last night's dinner went well, and his bird paintings sold for more than he even expected. Finch and Myles had arrived home the same time Parker got in. It was so nice without him here, Myles thought as he tried to finish the painting, a very standoffish kind of guy.

"A few more brush strokes and it's done," Myles now standing back to get a better look, placing his hand on his hip. "Beautiful," he concluded. "Now, for a little drying time."

"Myles are you in there?" called Finch, knocking on his door.

"Yes, one second Fresher," replied Myles as he turned his easel around not wanting Finch to see his work. "What's up," Myles continued as he opened his door.

"I have a couple more photos I took and wanted to know what you thought. Maybe you would like to paint these birds too." Finch excited to show Myles the pictures he downloaded to his phone.

"The birds are beautiful and again the background is very crisp as well. Definitely, these will do nicely," said Myles, with Finch smiling from ear to ear.

"Great I will send them to you on your phone. Gotta go, I'm meeting Megan for lunch and with school starting we have a few things to go over. Did you know she has never dated anyone and told me that she finds me very interesting? We like the same things, go figure. I wish my parents could meet her."

"Slow down Fresher, you just met her."

"I know Myles but sometimes you just know. When you click, it just feels right."

Myles thinking back how he felt about Louisa and how they met, marrying soon afterwards. Myles nodded and smiled. "You're right, somehow we just know, don't we? Enjoy your day, Fresher. Say hi to Megan for me, you do make a nice couple."

Finch left Myles and ran down the staircase not wanting to be late meeting Megan for lunch. "Whoa, where are you going in such a hurry?" Gage asked passing him in the front doorway.

"Meeting Megan, bye . . . oh, what happened to your hand?" Finch yelling as he ran to his car.

"It's all good, we'll talk later!" Gage grinned now knowing Finch's feelings for Megan were the same feelings he had for Raye. Maybe it was a mistake to get close to her, but his heart and head couldn't stop thinking about her. Even with her gone to the school today to help Laura and Tim Ashley being there, he wasn't concerned. He knew how Raye felt and if last night was any indication, he would have to think of her being a part of his life and fess up what he had been hiding. Hopefully she would see him in the same light.

With his hand all bandaged up there wasn't too much physically he could do. His nurse had told him to take the day off but Gage, being restless hosed his truck off and wiped it down, just taking his time using his good hand.

It was just him and Myles for lunch today and rather than sandwiches he was going to barbecue a few hotdogs. Gage headed upstairs to his room to change his damp shirt. Before closing his door behind him he could hear Myles talking to Sidney about staying in the box to sleep and that he would be right back. Gage smiled at how soft Myles was getting when it came to Sidney. If Myles went to his room for an afternoon nap Sidney was there at his door wanting to get in. It was getting to be such a regular thing that Myles would go get Sidney and take him upstairs. Myles was even calling him his little buddy.

Myles' door was partly open as he told Sidney to stay. He checked the hallway as he opened his door the rest of the way. Not seeing anyone he closed the door behind him while carrying the painting he had finished down the hallway to Mrs. Willoughby's room.

Taking a key from his pocket he entered the room, closing the door behind him. "What the bloody hell . . . oh, blimey . . . who would have done this?" he asked looking at the rummaged room. What were they looking for? he wondered as he gazed around the room seeing the painting still on the wall. Thank goodness he thought, as perspiration formed on his forehead while he carefully took the painting off the wall. With a skillful hand, he removed the original canvas and installed his own copy of the painting, placing it back on the wall. Good thing I'm replacing the painting with a phony one, he thought incase the person that did this comes back.

Now thinking they were going to get caught, Myles was scared not knowing what to do. He carefully picked up the painting and opened the door peering down the hallway. The coast was clear he thought as he closed Mrs. Willoughby's door and made it to his bedroom, hurrying inside.

"It was him all the time," Gage whispered to himself as he peeked through an open crack of his doorway. Maybe he had the money instead of Steve, he thought, not happy at knowing Myles was using his painting skills for a not so good cause. He was really beginning to like Myles and so was Raye. She will be devastated for sure and then there's Finch; poor Finch putting his trust and faith in a guy to help raise money for The National Audubon Society. What will the people who bought the paintings think?

Gage, feeling a little downhearted had to think of his next move. He had never let his feelings get the better of him; first Raye and now Myles. Was Gage becoming part of a new family? Loving grandparents had raised him after his mother died in childbirth. His grandfather taught him all he knew about renovating and the tools needed to do the job. Sadly, his grandfather died in his early fifties. His grandmother did her best but eventually became ill; needing a lot of care when Gage was eighteen, so he worked to make ends meet until she passed away a year later.

Gage left his room and knocked on Myles' door. "Hotdogs for lunch Myles, I'm putting the barbeque on?"

"Sure," said Myles. "I'll be right down. Let's go have lunch Sidney." Myles opened his door and escorted Sidney down the stairs and into the kitchen.

Gage already had the barbeque on with five hotdogs cooking as Myles joined him. It didn't take long, and they went inside to get the buns and condiments. Gage even cut up a hotdog for Sidney leaving two each for them. Gage could see there was something on Myles' mind. He looked pale and looked like he wanted to talk about it but refrained from doing so. Gage did most of the talking as Myles sat there eating his hotdog and just agreeing with whatever Gage said. Sidney was quite pleased with his and finished in record time, then off for another nap.

Gage took a bite of his hotdog loaded with sauerkraut. Myles had his usual mustard and relish. "Is everything all right?" Gage asked Myles. "You look a little upset."

"I'm okay, sometimes things don't go as we plan, but that's life."

Gage placed his hand on Myles' shoulder. "You know if you need anything, you just have to ask." Just as Myles nodded Gage's cell phone started ringing. Myles smiled as a country song played. "Hi, I'm glad you called. I thought you had a busy day. That was nice of Laura, tell her thank you. Yes, I haven't been using my sore hand. I'll take it easy. See you later, bye."

Myles sat there with his elbows bent and his hands together under his chin listening to the sweet talk. "Well, it's nice to see you finally realized what was right in front of you . . . you make a great couple, for sure."

As Gage cleared the dishes he agreed with Myles. "Don't think I didn't hear all those things you said under your breath when she was seeing that Tim guy. That was like a kick in the rear, for sure. So, thank you for that, Myles."

"You're welcome, anytime, now let me in there to wash those dishes," said Myles back to his old self.

"Absolutely, be my guest," said Gage as he stepped away giving Myles all the room he needed. Gage went out to the backyard not knowing what to do. Sitting around doing nothing was not something he enjoyed. He liked to keep busy, but he was under nurse Raye's strict orders, to do nothing.

Myles finished the dishes and headed to his room to figure out what to do. Should he put the painting back and the money that was sitting in a small bin under his bed? Mrs. Willoughby was coming home next week to see Myles and collect the painting. The bad guys wanted her painting, and she was only willing to give them the forgery that Myles had painted. He just had a feeling that things were going to go bad and needed to talk to her and warn her. Hopefully, it wasn't too late.

Myles picked up his phone and dialed her number. It rang and rang a few times before being answered. "Hello, Myles, is that you," said a sweet little voice that seemed concerned as to why Myles was calling. "Is there something wrong, dear?"

"Martha, I miss you very much. I wish you were here. We have a problem. I went into your room to exchange the painting, and someone has gone through your room, it's upside down. Someone was looking for something."

"Was the money in the safe that I left on my last visit?" asked Mrs. Willoughby, her voice becoming a little shaky, now thinking someone must be on to them.

"Yes luv, the room wasn't torn apart when I took it from the safe days earlier. But today when I went to exchange the paintings the room is turned upside down. They didn't take the painting so what were they looking for? Martha, it's not safe to come home," cautioned Myles not knowing what either of them could do.

The thought of Parker rummaging through her room entered his head. He looked like the kind of guy to do just that, getting his hands on anything that was valuable. Myles just realizing what he accused Parker of, was no different than what he was doing for money. Somehow though, what he was doing seemed more sophisticated than ransacking an old woman's room for money.

Martha on the other end of the phone was becoming upset herself, listening to Myles. Why now she wondered when her husband Arthur had been doing this for years? As curators of the museum Arthur started years ago with a priceless artifact that people just forgot about. He erased it from the books like it never existed. When the person that donated it to the museum died, Arthur made sure all traces of it were gone. After stealing one item it became two and two became three and so on. Eventually it became a game to Arthur. If he couldn't erase it, then it got lost or stolen. Even a small fire in the basement where some things were kept helped Arthur play his game that kept them quite wealthy.

When Arthur died, Martha wanted to make right what Arthur had done but didn't know how.

Arthur's connections were in England and when he died, the men who fenced his stolen goods weren't getting paid. Previously they were getting paid a percentage for everything they sold for Arthur. Now that he was gone, they decided to take over and told Mrs. Willoughby they were now in charge and that she was working for them. All the paintings, artifacts, jewellery and so much more that Arthur had accumulated throughout the years were stored away. With Arthur no longer running things, Mrs. Willoughby spent her time basically giving Arthur's treasure trove to the people now in charge.

By selling the house to Raye she was able to keep some of the things hidden within the house, things she hoped they would never find out about. Her Monet was one of the precious things she tried to hide, but somehow, they found out and wanted it.

She had met Myles at an auction selling a few of his paintings to help pay a debt after his wife passed away and she was looking for someone who could paint a Monet forgery. It was a union made in heaven as they both needed each other. The more time they spent together the more they fell in love. The hardest part was waiting until they saw each other. Finally, Raye renting a room to men allowed Myles to stay waiting for her to come home. But now even that was in jeopardy. Myles calling her had put himself in danger as well.

"I'm sorry, my love, I'm sorry I got you involved," she said, her voice expressing the passion in her heart. "It's not often people get a second chance to fall in love.

I miss you so much; I'll be home next week as planned, not to worry."

Myles felt better talking to Martha. All calmed down, he realized he just had to wait for her to come home and then it would be over. Like in the movies, they had planned to run away together where no one would find them, some warm exotic place to live out the rest of their lives. The Monet would be the first and last painting he would need to do for her. Myles, feeling more relaxed, sat down on his bed. "Should I tidy your room, luv?" asked Myles, waiting for a reply.

"That would be nice, thank you Myles. . . one second dear there's someone knocking at my door."

Myles listened as he heard her unlock the door. "What do you want?" she asked. "Yes, that's my name."

He heard a man's voice telling her she was under arrest then they were disconnected. Myles' heart pounded from his chest as he realized he would be next. The anxiety overwhelmed him as he sat on the edge of his bed thinking they would never be together as planned. Nowhere to hide and nowhere to run, all he could do now was wait.

Chapter 17

The noise in the room was set to a light murmur. Desks throughout the room were situated two at a time facing each other. The majority were on their computer or doing paperwork while the rest were talking amongst themselves. A medium build man with greying hair and a moustache dressed in a suit was detective Mark Lander. He sat down at one of the adjoining desks sitting across from a taller man, also with greying hair, detective Will Brady who was working very diligently on his computer. He was also dressed in a suit with his suit jacket hanging over the back of the chair.

"Fill me in," said Mark as he had been working on another case.

"Remember that hit and run we took on about a year ago and came up at a dead end."

"Yeah, the vehicle was never found. Didn't everyone die except the daughter?"

"Yes, that's the case. The crash vehicle caught fire and there was no evidence leading us to who did it. Well, it's been sitting on the back burner until weeks ago when the daughter called in and said she remembered seeing a logo on the truck door while in the back seat, probably flashbacks from the trauma. She was fortunate the two men passing by pulled her out before the car was engulfed in flames. I went to see her and had her pick the logo out from a list."

"Any luck?" asked Mark.

"Yeah, listen to this. The logo belongs to a construction company here in Bryerton called Wodale Co." Will said, quite enthused about hopefully ending the case.

"So, I guess I know where we're headed to."

"Yep, let's go, I'll drive," said Will grabbing his coat from the chair.

The drive only took ten minutes from the highway to an off ramp and down a tree lined street filled with industrial type businesses. Wodale Co. was at the end taking up a considerable amount of property with dump trucks, backhoes, excavators and loaders. Quite the business, Will thought as he pulled into the parking lot passing a few white company trucks. The logo on the driver's door was plain to see for sure.

"Do they know we're coming?" asked Mark before getting out of the car.

"No," said Will looking at Mark, "total surprise."

They got out of their car and headed to a building marked with a sign, office. Once inside they asked if they could speak to the manager or owner.

"Sure, one moment," said a young woman. She then went on an intercom to let the owner Cy Wodale know there were two men wanting to see him.

A broad medium sized man dressed in jeans and a T-shirt, wearing a hard hat and steel toed boots came into the office. Will noticed a two-way radio clipped to his waistband as the man entered taking off his hard hat placing his hand through his hair. "It must be important; we don't usually get suits here. What can I help you with?" Cy asked as he escorted the men to his office, closing the door behind them.

Both Will and Mark showed Cy their credentials before proceeding. Cy knew they were detectives just by the way they were dressed and their demeanor, very professional.

Cy's office was filled with family pictures and a very large aerial view of his land before the business had transpired. His desk was made of mahogany with a computer taking up one third of the space and mahogany bookshelves on the opposite wall. His office was nicely kept except for the papers strewn over the other two-thirds of his desk, thought Will as he looked the place over quickly, taking in anything that might seem unusual. Not wasting any time Will proceeded to let Cy know the reason for their visit.

"We recently have reason to believe one of your company trucks was in an accident about a year ago. "We would like to know who the driver of that vehicle was," Will said, already with a pen and paper in hand to write down the information, while Mark was there for backup letting Will ask most of the questions.

Cy went to his computer bringing up a folder called company truck repairs. In it was a list of all truck repairs dating back to when he first opened. "If it was in an accident, it should be listed in here because of the repairs needed . . . nothing," said Cy as he kept on looking. Scrolling down further, "Oh, wait, I do remember this; one of my drivers took a truck home the night before so he could be at the job site early the next morning to oversee some workers on a job and had to park the company vehicle off the property. When he went back to get the truck, he radioed in that it had been stolen. I remember now reporting it to the police and it was never found."

"The name of the driver would be helpful," said Will ready to write it down.

"The driver was Parker Tealson, nice kid, respectful and always trying to be helpful, but he no longer works for me. He quit and said he was moving. He was buddies with one of the guys still on my payroll, maybe they still keep in touch. One second and I'll ask him, he's washing one of the trucks, I should be able to get him on the two-way radio."

Cy took his radio from his waistband, seconds later one of his men answered. "Joe, for my records I was looking for the address of Parker Tealson. Is he still a friend of yours, I know he left a while back?"

Joe turned off the power hose to hear his boss more clearly. "Yeah, he moved out of town and rented a house with his brother in Turnersfield, 105 Waverly Road. But for some reason he's renting out a room at a rooming house. I didn't ask why and he's not much of a talker . . . awe, wait one second, I have it here on my phone . . . yeah, it's 17 Terry Lane in Turnersfield as well."

"Thanks Joe, and by-the-way good job yesterday with the crane. The Tierside Corporation was happy with the job you did. They will be asking for you again."

"Thanks boss, anytime."

Cy ended his call and looked at the two detectives. "I'm sure you got the addresses. If I can be of any more help, please let me know."

Will nodded as he opened his suit jacket and placed his pad and pen inside the pocket. "You have been very helpful," extending his hand out to Cy, with Mark doing the same. "We will stay in touch."

Will and Mark left the place feeling happy with the information they received, hoping the case was coming to a close. The next step was getting a warrant for the addresses, Will now realizing the last address was Miss Daniels. Why would Parker Tealson be renting a room from her? he wondered. Was he the hit and run driver and did Miss Daniels know him before she moved to Turnersfield? So many questions needed to be answered. Only going to Turnersfield would solve them. They headed back to the station; once the warrants were ready, they were off.

It was a quiet drive; traffic was steady but moving along nicely, no interruptions or clogged lanes. Heading to the off-ramp Will pointed out to Mark, who was on his phone texting, that they had reached Turnersfield. Will had turned on his GPS earlier, set to the address 105 Waverly Road. "Not far now," said Will looking at the final destination. Mark put his phone away looking for Waverly Road. "Just up ahead," said Will, now turning down the street then turning off his GPS.

"105, there it is," announced Mark looking the place over from a street view. It was a small bungalow with a separate garage. It was an older home that hadn't been taken care of. The grass needed to be cut, and the flower bed was nonexistent as weeds grew heartily within its border. Mark glanced at the garage, noticing a padlock on the door. "I wonder what's in there?"

"Well, good thing we have a warrant," said Will giving Mark a nod as he opened his car door. Mark followed Will going up the cracked sidewalk watching the front door as they got closer. Mark went over to the garage and looked in one of the dirt-covered windows. Mark nodded to Will, sure enough there was a white pickup truck in the garage. Mark took out his cell phone, talked briefly to someone then hung-up joining Will at the front door as he rang the door bell.

The door opened with Steve standing there with a surprised look on his face. "What do you want?" he asked them with a snide look.

"Does Parker Tealson live here?" asked Will as Mark just stared at Steve.

"No, not now . . . I mean he did . . . but he's gone," said Steve now beginning to ramble on.

"Who are you?" asked Mark, still watching Steve's body movements.

"I'm his brother Steve . . . what's this all about anyways?"

"I'm detective Will Brady and this is detective Mark Lander," Steve backed up as they showed their credentials.

"We have a warrant to search the property, open the garage door and if you're thinking about running, I will save you the notion. The Turnersfield police are on there way."

Steve opened the garage door shaking in his shoes. Will and Mark looked on, once opened the three of them entered the garage. The logo on the door of the truck now confirmed it did indeed belong to the Wodale Co. The company truck had the whole front end smashed in. "I wasn't driving it, it was all my brother, I didn't have anything to do with it, it was his idea." Steve sold his brother out before the detectives could ask any questions.

The local Police had just shown up, one of the two officers went to talk to Will while the other stood there listening to Steve.

After talking to Will the police officer went over to Steve and arrested him for an accessory after the fact to an offence and for obstructing justice. He handcuffed Steve and after telling him his rights the two officers escorted him to the police cruiser.

Mark called his police station in Bryerton to have a forensic unit come out to look over the truck and positively make sure it was the vehicle involved in the collision. They needed to identify any paint chips found on the truck that would match the make and model of Raye's parent's car. Anything that would tie the truck into the crash during that night. They also needed the fingerprints of the person driving the truck.

The police cruiser was ready to take Steve in and called another cruiser to meet the detectives at 17 Terry Lane. It was late afternoon, and they didn't know if Parker would be at this address or not. "Please ask them to park on the roadway out of site. We don't want to scare him off if he is on his way home," said Will hoping everything would go according to plan.

Will and Mark headed to Raye's house while Will filled Mark in about Raye and how she can be very vulnerable. "She's been waiting for this a long time, and I don't know how she is going to take it knowing Parker has been in her house the whole time. I'm still not sure why he would want to live there. The pieces should soon come together."

"Wow, quite the house," said Mark as Will pulled in the driveway and parked the car.

"Yes, if I remember correctly, it is just as beautiful inside too."

They made their way to the front door and used the door knocker. It only took a minute, and the door opened with Raye standing on the other side. "Hello, detective Brady, what are you doing here?" she asked looking at the other man.

"Miss Daniels, this is my partner detective Mark Landers. May we come in?"

"Yes of course, forgive me, I don't get very many visitors. What's this visit about?" asked Raye as Gage made his way to the foyer in case he needed her. "This is Gage Manning, and oh," as she looked towards Gage, she saw Finch and Myles coming to see what was going on too. Raye smiled as she introduced Finch Edwards and Myles Culpepper to the detectives. Myles was ready as he thought they were here to arrest him.

"Nice to meet all of you, I do remember meeting Gage and Finch the last time I came to see you. You have a very nice support group, Miss Daniels," said Will as Mark stared at Gage.

"Your name seems familiar . . . no maybe not . . . maybe it will come to me, however it's nice to meet all of you too," said Mark still trying to associate Gage's name.

Raye had them all sit in the living room where everyone would be more comfortable.

So, what's this all about?" she asked again.

"Do you have a tenant called Parker Tealson?"

"No, detective Brady, a Parker Cleve. Tealson is the last name of my ex-boyfriend."

Raye got up from her chair as her face changed to one of realization, her hand covered her mouth in distress. "You mean Parker and Steve are brothers?"

Gage was as surprised as Finch and Myles looking at each other in disbelief.

"I'm afraid so, Miss Daniels. Steve Tealson was arrested an hour ago and the truck used in the crash was hidden in his garage. We came here to arrest Parker for the murder of your parents. We're pretty sure Parker was the one driving the truck that hit your parent's car."

Raye took a deep breath releasing all the built-up stress knowing the person had been found that ruined her life. Gage sitting beside her held her hand giving it a little squeeze to try and comfort her. "But why would Parker rent a room from me; it doesn't make sense?"

"I don't know," said detective Brady, we will get a lot of answers eventually.

"My partner would like to check out his room if you don't mind."

"Yes, of course, I'll get the spare key," said Raye, going to the den to get it.

A few minutes later she handed it to detective Lander and Finch showed him which room was Parker's. He did a quick search as Finch stood there and watched. Leaving everything intact they headed back to the living room. They all stopped talking as Finch and detective Lander entered the room. "It's clean, nothing but his clothes. We'll send the forensic team to pick them up when they come to look at the truck. For now, just leave everything the way it is."

Raye nodded, detective Brady noticing she was becoming a little unsettled. Just then his phone rang.

"Yes, we will be right out." Will Brady looked at Raye regaining her composure and told her that her worries were over and that the Turnersfield police were outside arresting Parker Tealson in her driveway. He won't be bothering you anymore."

They all headed to the front door to see for themselves. They put Parker in handcuffs and into the cruiser then drove away.

"They will be back to impound his car, Miss Daniels. Sorry, there wasn't an easier way to tell you. I hope you can get some peace of mind now that the person has been found. We should be going, and in the future, there will be some people getting a hold of you when it comes to trial."

"Thank you, for everything you and your colleague have done. But one question, why was Steve arrested?"

"We don't know for sure Miss Daniels; he may have been in the truck as well. I think it was only Parker. However, he knew what Parker had done so he was an accessory to the crime, plus he helped hide the vehicle."

"Thank you again for everything you've done," said Raye grasping tightly onto Gage's hand.

Detective Brady smiled looking at Raye. "It was really you that solved the case by seeing the logo. It was you that put all the pieces together. Now you can rest assure that your parents are at peace knowing it's over too. Live each day fully Miss Daniels, and don't stop remembering the good times," said detective Brady as he and detective Lander headed out the front door. "Goodbye."

Chapter 18

The night was full of questions as they all looked dumbfounded, not believing what had transpired. They all sat at the kitchen island staring into space. Raye opened two bottles of wine pouring a glass for everyone. "I guess it's a bittersweet celebration," she said as she looked at the others numb at what had transpired.

"Thanks, luv, I can certainly use this," said Myles as he drank back half the glass. Now knowing Martha had been arrested, he was waiting for his turn thinking they had come for him. It was only a matter of time, thinking maybe he should tell them and get it over with. It would certainly surprise everyone, since they had become like family to him.

Parker had everyone fooled as well, except for his miserable disposition. Raye was in-between happy and upset. She was in disbelief more so than the rest of them, it was so surreal she thought. Finally, she could carry on knowing justice would be done. But the disturbing thing was Steve. "Gage, why didn't I feel something inside to warn me about Steve being a predator?" Both Finch and Myles looked at Gage waiting for his answer.

"I think your mind was still processing the accident. Like detective Brady said, you put all the pieces together. Your mind has been showing you, it just took time. So, when a friendly face like Steve came along that you could cling to, you grabbed onto it. Also, if it's anything we all have learned knowing you is that you can't conceive anyone being mean. It's not in you, so you don't think that people can use others for an ulterior motive. You Raye Daniels are a very good person."

Gage took a sip of his wine feeling bad since he hadn't been completely truthful to her either. All he could hope for was her understanding.

"Well, I guess we should look on the bright side," said Finch also drinking back the wine. "You can rent his room out to someone nice, someone that we will all get along with. Someone who likes birds, maybe."

They all laughed looking at Finch. "Are you daft Fresher? Isn't one Finch enough?" commented Myles. Finch taking another sip of wine realized Myles was right.

"I am one of a kind for sure, Myles."

Myles looked up from his glass. "You are that Fresher, you are that." Raye and Gage looked at each other smiling.

"Could I get more wine luv?" asked Myles getting up the nerve to tell them what he had been doing. Because he considered them family, he didn't want them trying to figure stuff out later. They deserved an explanation. Was he ready for the hurtful things they might say? It didn't matter it was time to be honest.

Myles picked up his glass and made a toast, the rest listening attentively. "I want to tell you that you all have made me feel like family. Since my Louisa passed away, I haven't had that. For a while I felt very lonely and when she passed, she left me with a lot a debt that I was unable to pay for."

"Oh my," said Finch showing empathy towards Myles and his hardships.

"Thanks Fresher, but I'm not telling all of you this to get any sympathy. Please let me go on I don't know how much time I have."

"Sure," said Gage looking over at Raye. "We are here for you; take all the time you need." Gage poured himself another glass of wine and topped up everyone else's.

Myles continued . . . "I had a lot of my paintings I could sell to help my finances; so, I auctioned them off. While at the auction I met a lady named Martha; Martha Willoughby."

Raye put down her glass not believing what she was about to hear, pulling her chair closer to Gage, holding on to his hand. Raye wanting to ask questions sat there in silence as did the rest.

"The woman I met was beautiful, sophisticated, a little bossy in a good way and very kind. She needed someone to paint and I needed cash, a lot of cash. It was a win-win for both of us but then the unexpected happened. We fell in love with each other and felt blessed to have found love a second time." Myles, teary eyed got up and stood on the other side of the island, looking at them in remorse.

"I'm telling you this because Martha has been arrested. The police in London have caught on to her and it is just a matter of time before I'm arrested too."

Finch, not waiting until the end wanted to know what she was arrested for and what it was that Myles did for her.

"Fresher . . . Martha and her husband were the curators for The Fine Arts Museum in Turnersfield. Her husband was stealing paintings and artifacts plus anything else he could steal for cash and not get caught. When Arthur died, Martha didn't want to sell Arthur's stolen goods, but the seller or middle guy wouldn't let her quit or he would report her and maybe he did, I don't know. They were blackmailing her to keep giving them the stolen items so they could make a profit. The one thing she cared about the most was a Monet painting her husband gave to her on their wedding day. That painting he gave her was not stolen, he actually paid for it before he became curator. The blackmailers knew she had it and wanted it. This is why she wanted me especially as a painter because like Gage had already guessed I paint like Monet. She wanted me to make a forgery for the Monet painting in her room, which I did. The original is in my room worth millions."

Raye got up from her chair and walked over to Myles and gave him a hug. "I'm not condoning what you have done but I understand why. But surely you must have known you would have gotten caught eventually."

Myles wiped a tear from his eye and nodded. "I took one day at a time not thinking of the consequences. I only knew what I was going through after Louisa died was not living. Martha gave me hope, she gave me a reason to carry on. What was going to happen after that didn't matter. I was finally happy plus living here and meeting all of you. I will never forget any of you." Myles looked over at Finch while biting his lip trying to get the words out. "I will miss you most of all Fresher, and the meetings we went to. I'm sorry I won't be able to paint any more pictures for you unless I can paint in jail."

Myles looked over at Gage, wondering why he hadn't asked any questions. "No, questions Gage?"

Gage looked at Myles for a second then asked, "Why don't you run, Myles. Leave tonight while you can?"

Myles stood there thinking and looking at the three of them. "First, I have nowhere to run to, my home is here now. Second, I would have no one to spend my life with, I would just be alone and third I would miss you guys terribly. At least in jail you might come and visit me."

"Well then," said Raye thinking of how they could make his last night special. She went into the cupboards and pulled out two more bottles of wine. "You're in charge of these," she said as she handed them to Gage. She then went into the pantry and pulled out chips and cheese puffs and handed them to Finch. "Here Finch, open these and put them in bowls . . . oh, and maybe you would like to call Megan to come over too. Myles, you're on popcorn duty, here you go," giving Myles two packages of microwavable popcorn.

Everyone was looking at Raye like she had lost her mind. "What?" she said looking at all of them. "We can't throw Myles a going away party unless we have drinks and food. Oh . . . and I'll cook a couple of pizzas, which should do nicely. Now for music, can you help me out Gage?"

Gage thought it was a great idea, nodding his head and smiling. He loved that girl more and more each day. While Myles and Finch were busy with the snacks and watching the pizza Raye put in the oven, she took some flyers from her recycling bin and started folding them. Gage looked on as she finished. "Here, one for you," she said to Myles as she put a paper hat on his head, "and one for you Finch plus one for Megan." Gage smiled as she approached him with a hat as well. "I saved the best for you," she whispered in his ear as the wine was starting to have an effect on her.

Raye grabbed her hat while they all carried something outside, placing it on the patio table. Gage and Myles picked up the table and moved it over to the side of the patio so there was room for dancing. Megan and Raye took turns dancing with Myles. Then Megan and Finch danced to a few fast songs. Gage played a variety of songs but made sure that he saved a few slow ones that he liked for him and Raye. A slow song started as Finch and Megan wrapped their arms around each other, Gage having the same idea.

"I think this is our dance," Gage said as he came up behind Raye and put his arms around her. Raye turned around and smiled as she put her arms around his neck looking into his eyes. "Be careful of your hand Mr. Manning, don't hold on too tight now." Gage laughed as he pulled her closer. He just couldn't get enough of her. The smell of her hair was intoxicating. It smelled like the lavender plant in the flowerbed but lightly scented with the sweet smell of honey, leaving you wanting more.

"This was a nice thing you did for Myles. I was surprised he told us everything."

"Yeah, me too," said Raye, "especially after what happened with Parker and Steve. I still can't believe they were brothers. Do you think the two of them being arrested made him want to be honest with us?"

"Probably . . . and because we mean a lot to him, like he said, were family. I think he is just a lonely old man wanting to belong like the rest of us. He did it to pay off his bills and fell in love. Does he regret it? Yes, but we have to learn from our mistakes. He is a better man than some, for sure. But the law is the law. Bye the way, there is something I need to tell you . . ."

"My turn, I'm cutting in, you've had her long enough," announced Myles wanting a turn dancing with Raye.

Myles had a few swerves and dips in his slow dancing which reminded Raye of her dad when they used to dance together. He taught her how to dance so she wouldn't be embarrassed at her high school prom. He was a very smooth dancer like Myles. The music stopped and Myles hugged Raye. "Thank you for tonight, Raye. I will never forget this night."

Raye smiled and gave Myles a hug, "I will never forget it either and I will come and visit you. You won't be forgotten and if I can bring you paint supplies, I will. What makes you think they will come tomorrow?"

Myles and Raye sat down leaving Finch and Megan still dancing. "I called Martha and now they have her cell phone and anyone she has been talking to. It's only a matter of time."

The party went on until two in the morning. Everyone had an emotional day and enjoyed Myles' going away party. They all went to their respective rooms except Megan. Raye and Megan bunked together leaving Gage a little disgruntled.

Chapter 19

No one got up before ten. It was a warm sunny morning with a beautiful breeze coming through the patio doors. Raye and Megan were up first making coffee and brunch. The smell of freshly brewed coffee should wake them up for sure they thought or maybe the smell of pancakes. The aroma of the cooked bacon was filling the house as well, even though the vent hood was on.

The first guy to walk through the doorway was Finch with a smile on his face as soon as he saw Megan. He walked over and gave her a good morning kiss then poured himself a coffee. "Mmm . . ." he said taking a sip as he sat down at the table. "Nothing like a cup of coffee, does anyone have something for a headache?"

"You mean a hangover," said Raye, "you'll feel better once you eat."

Just then the other two came into the kitchen, both looking like a bus hit them. Both holding their heads and squinting at the light. "Sit down you two," Raye chuckled placing a coffee in front of each of them. "Here be careful it's quite hot."

Gage looked at Raye trying to give her a smile. "You drank as much as we did, how come you're doing fine and Megan too?"

"We both switched to water an hour before bed, I made sure of that. I guess you guys missed the memo," laughed Raye actually feeling sorry for them. "You both need to eat something, what would you like, pancakes, bacon or scrambled eggs . . . Gage . . . Myles?" Megan had already taken care of Finch with the two of them sitting next to each other at the kitchen table.

Gage lifted his head from his hand. "A little of everything would be nice, thank you."

"Yeah, that sounds about right for me too," said Myles, "and thank you . . . for everything."

Raye made up their plates and placed them in front of them, then making a plate for herself. She sat in between Gage and Myles drinking a peppermint tea she had made for herself. "So, I was thinking," taking a look at Gage then Myles, "how about we keep the party going and. . ."

Just those words were enough for Myles and Gage to look at Raye. "We're wounded here can't you see; we have nothing left."

"Yeah," said Myles, "if we can do it maybe tomorrow, I'm all for it but more dancing, I don't think so."

"Oh, stop the both of you," said Raye laughing, "I don't mean a drinking, dancing kind of party, just something we can all do together."

When Finch heard that he couldn't wait to express his idea, "Why don't we all go bird watching, Myles will love it and you can all see first hand what it is Megan and I do. It's not strenuous; you mostly sit and wait once you get to a good area. All you need is food, water and a chair . . . oh and a hat would be good."

Megan smiled, nodding her head. "Finch and I could take more pictures to help out with the bird photography portfolio we are doing together for this area."

The three of them looked at each other. Raye was in, raising her eyebrows and smiling at the other two. Myles, finally taking his hand from his head, was thinking at least he could sit in a chair in the fresh air and not have to do anything while Gage was thinking it would be a nice send off for Myles. They both looked at each other and grinned. "I'm in," they said, knowing it was going to be another long day.

"Great," said Raye now standing, taking her empty plate to the sink. "Finish up, there's more coffee and still a pancake or two if anyone is interested." Myles right away jumped on having the last ones. It seems he was feeling better as Raye quickly put them on his plate. Then Raye turned to Gage. "I would like to see your hand before we go," with Gage nodding an affirmative.

It didn't take long for everyone to clear the kitchen except for Raye and Gage. Raye had cleaned up and did the dishes while chasing everyone out except Gage. She had her first aide kit handy and went over to Gage, sitting at the island beside him. "Let me see how your hand is doing." Raye gently took off the gauze. "Hmm ... it's healing nicely. No more wrapping it up." Raye smiled looking at Gage. "You've been a very good patient."

"Well thank you nurse Raye . . . oh wait . . . let me thank you properly." Gage got up and took Raye by the hand pulling her to his chest, embracing her and placing his lips on hers. The kiss was a long, sensuous kiss leaving Raye wanting more. They headed to her bedroom, closing the door behind them. Gage pulled the bed spread from the bed as Raye started undressing longing to feel his touch.

"Wait let me help you." he said as he stripped off his clothes eagerly leaving his strong well-built stature exposed. He helped undc her bra and slipping her panties down, letting them drop to the floor as he ran his hand along her breasts then kissed her passionately. Gage embraced Raye, picking her up and placing her onto the bed, then placing his body on top of her as they both sank deeper into the sheets.

With his muscular arms he held himself up kissing her neck and running his lips over her breasts and beyond. Raye found his sexual pleasure stimulating as their body heat melded together sending her into a kaleidoscope of complete satisfaction. Both were being considerate of each other's vulnerabilities, taking pleasure embracing the feeling they had for one another. They were two now becoming one as their hearts raced pounding the heightened gratification of their intimate connection.

Gage placed his body beside Raye's as she placed her head on his chest. They both caressed each other in total gratification laying there relaxed in each other's arms.

Finch and Megan were packing Finch's car with their cameras and a cooler filled with sandwiches they made once the kitchen was clear. Megan made lemonade from cans that Raye had mentioned were in the freezer. All she had to do was add water and ice.

Myles went back to bed to have a nap with Sidney curled up in his cardboard box. Myles had asked Finch to wake him when it was time to leave.

Raye, realizing they had to get ready, told Gage she was going to take a shower. Gage thought he would have one too and followed her into the bathroom. Raye turned around looking at him wrinkling her brow in confusion.

"We can save time if we shower together," he said waiting for a nod of approval.

She smiled. "You're right," she said opening the shower door looking at Gage. "Just a quick shower and were done, they'll be waiting for us."

Gage hesitated, smiled then agreed, stepping into the shower unable to take his eyes off Raye. The silhouette of her body was irresistible as he kissed the side of her neck and slid his lips down to her shoulders, caressing her breasts.

"Now, stop that, you agreed," she laughed trying to lather up and finish her shower. "Here, let me get your back."

Gage turned around as she lathered his back, then handed him the soap as she stepped out of the shower. She grabbed a towel as drops of water ran down her body. Once dry she towel dried her hair then went into the bedroom to get dressed. Gage finished, came out of the bathroom with a towel wrapped around his waist watching Raye. She put on a lacy bra and a silky pair of panties. Next, she put on a long-sleeved T-shirt in case of bugs and a pair a jeans; this being her second ensemble for the day. She fixed her hair pinning up the sides as the short bob was now almost chin length. No blush was needed as the permanent smile on her face made her glow. Finished, she looked at Gage smiling at her. "What . . . what's going on in that mind of yours?"

"Oh nothing, I was just thinking how lucky I was to find you."

"I feel the same way. Now you, Mister, need to get dressed. Would you like me to get you some clothes from your room, Gage?"

"Thanks, that would be great, here's the key. Just a t-shirt and a pair of jeans . . . oh, and my cell phone too. I think I left it on my bedside table."

"Okay, I'll be right back," said Raye as she left and went up stairs to his room. Reaching the staircase, she saw Myles at the top wondering why no one had woken him up.

"We're all still getting ready," she said climbing the stairs and reaching the top, now standing in front of Myles. "I need some clothes for Gage, and I saw Finch and Megan taking things out to his car. Are you taking a sketch book and some paints with you Myles?"

"Oh yes, thank you, luv," said Myles, still a little groggy from his sleep.

Raye unlocked the door and went into Gage's room as Myles looked on rubbing his head wondering why Gage needed clothes and couldn't get them himself. "Probably another one of Raye's memos that no one got," he chuckled to himself as he walked back to his room. "Come on Sid, you've been here all morning, you haven't even eaten today."

Sidney stretched as he watched Myles collecting his art kit and sketch book filled with paper that he could use different mediums on; one of his favourites was oil pastels. With everything he needed and Sidney following he closed his door and headed to the stairs hearing Raye in Gage's room. "Let's go find the others," he told Sidney as he followed Myles down the stairs and into the kitchen.

Raye closed the dresser drawer carrying a T-shirt and jeans. "Now, where can his phone be," she said as she laid his clothes on the bed. "Maybe in here," opening the drawer of his bedside table. "What the . . . what the heck, why would he have a gun?" All of a sudden, her mind went to the news program she had listened to, telling the public about a dangerous man that the police were looking for in Hamden Shore. I can't believe it she thought almost in tears wondering what to do pacing back and forth. He'll wonder why I'm taking so long she thought closing the drawer. Now where is that phone of his, lifting up his pillow. "There you are," she said aloud, grabbing his clothes before she left his room closing the door behind her.

"We're leaving soon!" Finch yelled to Raye seeing her coming down the staircase as he was in the foyer heading to the front door. Raye nodded, walking quickly to give Gage his clothes and to get her phone so she could call detective Brady. First Steve then Parker and now Gage she thought as she entered her room noticing the bed was made and everything tidy.

"Here you go, it was under your pillow," she said, handing Gage the phone and his clothes. "I ran into Myles and Finch; we will be leaving soon and thanks for tidying up."

"You're welcome and thanks for the clothes," Gage said as he undid the towel from his waist and slipped on his jeans then putting on his T-shirt. "I'll go and see if I can help the guys."

Raye needing a minute, smiled and nodded giving him a quick kiss as he left the room not wanting Gage to suspect she knew about the gun. She took her phone from her top dresser drawer and remembered detective Brady had given her his number in case she needed to get in touch with him, this way she could call him directly.

Closing the door, she sat on the bed dialing his number. It rang a few times then his voicemail came on. She really wanted to talk to him on the phone and not leave a message. She would call him later she thought, hanging up. Just then her phone rang. "Hello, yes hello detective Brady. Do you remember my friend Gage Manning?"

"Yes, your handyman. Is there something wrong?"

"I found a gun in his room; I think he's the guy they're looking for in Hamden Shore. I saw the news broadcast that they were looking for a guy and Gage fits the description. I didn't really think it was him until I found the gun, now I'm not so sure." Raye's voice was now quivering as she got up from the bed pacing the floor waiting for a response.

"Calm down, Miss Daniels. I need to put you on hold for a moment, please wait on the line."

Raye, thinking that Gage was going to come through the door any minute wanted to hide. She took the phone with her into the bathroom and shut the door, turning on the water just in case.

"Miss Daniels."

"Yes, detective Brady, I'm here."

"The man you're referring to on the news was found and arrested and is in police custody. Mr. Manning is not that man. Also, it is not unusual for someone to own a gun. You have nothing to worry about. I hope I have settled any fears you have."

"Yes, thank you detective Brady. It's good news and thank you for getting back to me so quickly. Lately my mind jumps to conclusions."

"That's quite understandable; if you ever need to call again, please don't hesitate. Goodbye, Miss Daniels."

"Thank you, goodbye."

Raye turned off the water and exited the bathroom, still a little unnerved and upset with herself thinking the worst. She sat on the bed thinking maybe she should have confronted Gage and gave him the benefit of the doubt.

Just then Gage came in and asked her what was taking her so long because everyone was ready to go. Noticing the sad look on her face he asked her, "What's wrong, is everything okay?"

Her eyes were teary-eyed as she stood up looking at Gage. Then she gave Gage a kiss and a hug, not wanting to let go.

"We can stay if you want," he laughed as Raye looked at him and smiled. "Let's go," he said holding her hand leading the way.

Raye got into Gage's truck with his help and Myles went with Finch and Megan. The sun was still shining high in the sky giving warmth to anything in its path. Each patch of woodlands they passed; Myles thought their journey had ended. "How much longer, Fresher?" he would ask being impatient instead of enjoying the ride.

Thirty minutes later Finch pulled off the main road and took a dirt road into a woodsy area. The trees were tall with an assortment of different varieties and shrubs everywhere. There was a slight clearing ahead where

Finch pulled in and parked his car with Gage pulling up along side of him.

They all got out of their cars with Myles already complaining. "Well, we're sure out in no mans land, Fresher."

Finch smiled as he opened his trunk taking out the chairs, handing two to Gage and one to Megan while he took his and Myles'. "We'll get the cooler once we're settled," he said to Gage.

They all walked single file through the long grass and succulents with Finch leading the way. Everyone had their hats on carrying their chairs except for Myles as he had his art supplies to carry plus his umbrella.

"Let's set up here," Finch said with Megan agreeing. The rest opened their chairs and sat down, now taking a good look at their surroundings. They could see why Finch picked this spot. There were a few smaller trees nestled beside each other in the surrounding area. Finch and Megan set up their cameras in front of their chairs which were in direct line with the trees. Any birds that landed in one of those trees would be photographed for sure. It was all in timing.

Myles moved his chair ahead of everyone else closer to a bush hoping a bird would land there and stay long enough for him to sketch it then colour from memory. Even just a sketch of the scenery would be nice, he thought as he looked over at his new family. Myles did one sketch after the other as he took a few bites of a sandwich that Megan had given him along with a glass of lemonade.

Myles glanced over at the four of them laughing and pointing at the birds hoping they would land in the trees for Finch and Megan to get some pictures. "I'm going to miss you all," he said to himself smiling at how they all got along; thinking of the dances he had with Raye and Megan and going to the meeting with Fresher and helping Gage put up the bird houses.

This was his last night as he couldn't wait any longer wondering when they were going to come for him. Tomorrow morning, he was going to turn himself in and let them know tonight so he could say his goodbyes. Plus, he didn't want Raye to plan any more surprises, always trying to make others happy. It had been a wonderful two days he would never forget.

The sun was going down and they packed up carrying everything to their vehicles. Finch and Megan took so many beautiful pictures of a variety of different birds. The drive home seemed much quicker than going. It must be the anticipation of wanting to get to the destination making it seem longer.

Finch pulled into the driveway with Gage and Raye right behind them. Myles got out of the car and waited for everyone else. "I have something I would like to say." The four of them stood together waiting for Myles to continue. "Tomorrow morning, I'm turning myself in."

"Myles," said Gage and the others adding their vocal displeasure.

"Now, now, that's the way it's going to be, it's what I want. So, in case I don't see you all, especially you Megan, it's been a pleasure luv. Take care of my Fresher."

"I will," said Megan giving Myles a hug then getting into her car, waving as she pulled out. The rest went inside giving Myles a hug goodnight, telling him they would be there for him in the morning.

Chapter 20

Everyone was up early except Myles. No one could actually sleep thinking all night long of what had transpired last night. The three of them were in the kitchen having coffee not saying a word, just staring into their cup.

A country song started playing as Finch and Raye looked over at Gage. Gage answered his phone as he went out to the patio closing the doors behind him. "Eric, how's everything at the other end."

"It's all been taken care of. I'll see you later today. Just call."

Gage hung up his phone and went back inside. Finch and Raye were talking about Finch starting his courses tomorrow. He was getting anxious about a couple of his classes but having Megan in all but one was a big plus. They could help each other and having a study partner would be a good thing as well.

"Is anyone hungry?" Raye asked, not being able to sit still knowing Myles was going to turn himself in today. "I'm making pancakes, this time Myles' number one favourite, chocolate chip."

"Count me in," said Gage looking over at Finch. "Finch, buddy, do you want some pancakes?" asked Gage.

"Oh yeah, sorry . . . I just can't believe Myles is leaving."

Gage looked at his watch, then at Raye, then at Finch.

"Do you think he's already left?" asked Raye.

"That's exactly what I was wondering myself. I'm going to his room to check." Gage got up heading to the staircase. Climbing the stairs his heart was pumping fiercely thinking Myles had left. He reached the hallway and stood outside Myles' door. Sidney was sitting there waiting to go in. Gage didn't want to knock on the door in case he was still in bed asleep, but he wanted to know if he was still in there. Gage stood there not knowing what to do.

"Good morning, Gage, what are you doing?" asked Myles, coming down the hall from the bathroom.

"I came up to see if you were awake, to let you know Raye was making your favourite, chocolate chip pancakes."

"I'm sure she is Gage but we both know why you came up. You didn't know if I was still here."

Gage half smiled and nodded his head. "You're right, and I wanted to talk to you about that. Can we talk?"

"Sure, come on in," said Myles opening his door and closing it behind Gage.

Sidney was still sitting there as Myles shut his door. Not waiting any longer, he headed to the kitchen hoping there was a piece of bacon or a slice of ham sitting on a plate waiting for him. He went over to his dish and beside his kibble bowl was a plate with broken pieces of bacon. "Good morning pretty boy, where have you been all night?" Raye picked up Sidney and gave him a kiss on the head and placed him back on the floor.

Finch watched as Raye gave Sidney some affection. "He's got you tied around his paw for sure." They both laughed because it was true and Finch knew it because he did the same thing to his cat Ollie.

Raye and Finch had already started on their pancakes. Since Gage hadn't returned, they both figured that Myles was still here. Raye made quite a few pancakes and placed them in the warming tray.

Raye got up to get herself another coffee. "Would you like some more, Finch?" she asked, looking at him with the percolator in her hand.

"Sure thanks, the more caffeine the better; I have a lot of photos to download and look through on my laptop."

Raye smiled pouring Finch more coffee. "You picked a great spot; we all enjoyed it so much and I'm sure Myles did a lot of nice sketches."

"Yes, I did," said Myles standing at the doorway with Gage right behind him.

"Good morning, Myles, take a seat and I'll get you a coffee."

"Thank you, luv, but would you mind if I had a tea this morning, it makes me think of home and a few of those lovely smelling pancakes too, I hope." Myles tilted his head back slightly, taking in a deep breath smelling the aroma in the air with exaggerated pleasure.

Raye smiled and nodded, then asked Gage as well. "Yes, two please and a refill on the coffee if you don't mind."

Raye was happy that Myles didn't sneak out in the middle of the night. It showed her that he was a man of his word and thought enough of them to wait until morning. Another member of the family walked through the kitchen door. Megan had come to see Myles off as well. "I couldn't stay away," looking at Myles. "I know we said our goodbyes, but I just wanted another hug, I guess."

Myles got up and gave her a hug and thanked her, then he looked over at Finch. "This one's a keeper, Fresher, treat her right." Finch smiled and nodded looking at Megan as she came and sat down beside him.

Raye served her a coffee, but Megan had already eaten breakfast and declined the pancakes. Myles had taken his last bite and handed his plate to Raye thanking her again for making them, then taking a sip of his tea he slowly put down his cup and told everyone that he had something to say. "The police will be here within the hour, probably already on there way."

Everyone was getting teary-eyed, especially Raye as she went over to hug him. "Oh, now look what you have gone and done," said Myles wiping his eyes with his napkin.

Finch started talking about the different birds that they took pictures of yesterday and even a few baby birds he spotted in a nest. He told Myles that if he is allowed his phone that he would send him some of the pictures when he got them downloaded. If not, he would visit him and show him then.

Just then a knock, knock, knock at the front door. That was the first time Raye didn't want to hear the door knocker which would now remind her of another sad day.

"I'll get it," said Gage as he got up to answer the door. "Good morning, right this way," he motioned to the policemen taking them into the kitchen. They were both dressed in plain clothes with badges and there was another cruiser outside with the officers dressed in uniform. Gage introduced all of them leaving Myles last.

"Mr. Myles Culpepper," said the one police officer as Myles stood up and turned his back to him placing his arms behind him. "I think we can forgo the handcuffs please turn around." The officer told him his rights and thanked him for making this easy for everyone involved.

They walked Myles to the front door letting him give one last hug to Raye, Megan and Finch. As he hugged Gage he whispered in his ear, "Thank you."

The officers opened the front door as the two uniformed officers standing outside took Myles and escorted him to their cruiser. Myles looked back as they asked him to get into the back seat, closing the door behind him. The group was now outside waving as the police cruiser left. Finch and Megan didn't see any need staying and went to her room over the diner to get ready for their big day tomorrow on campus.

As they left a van came up the driveway pulling up as close as they could to the front door. One man and one woman dressed in police uniform got out and talked to the two men in street clothes who waved Gage over. Gage shook hands with the two in uniform and gave them something from his pocket.

Raye stood there wondering what was going on as Gage seemed to be getting very friendly with all of them. Gage went to Raye to fill her in what was going to happen next. "I gave them Myles' key so they could search his room and confiscate anything that was stolen, as well as the Monet painting in his room and the money that Mrs. Willoughby gave him. Let's go to the backyard and sit on the patio, there is more I need to tell you."

Raye nodded as he took her hand and led her to the side gate and into the backyard. Once she was sitting down, he knew he had to tell her the truth. Gage was pacing back and forth not knowing what to say. "Please have an open mind and please don't be upset with me, Raye."

Raye knew he was worried, the perspiration on his forehead was an obvious indication. "Just tell me."

Gage looked at her and spilled it out all at once, getting it off his chest. "I'm an undercover cop and my job was to come here and rent a room and be your handyman because the department has been on to Mrs. Willoughby for some time, and we needed to know who her accomplices were, unfortunately her living here made you also a suspect."

"What . . . what . . . I can't believe this . . . you thought I was a thief!" Raye was fit to be tied as she started to pace back and forth.

"No, not once I got to know you better, I didn't think you were. Your boyfriend became a suspect. Pretty much everyone in the house became a suspect. I was just doing my job. Eventually I found out it was Myles. We knew Mrs. Willoughby was being blackmailed just like Myles said but we needed to wait and see if we could get the blackmailers, and we did."

"So that's why you didn't want to make a commitment because you thought I was involved . . . you thought I was a bad person." Raye shook her head looking at Gage in disgust. "You made me think you were some guy down on his luck and needed a place to stay. I fell in love with you, and you used me."

"No," said Gage wanting to hold her, "I tried not to fall in love with you. I tried so hard that the thought of you and Tim made me upset and then all the walls came down. My armour was stripped . . . I'm in love with you, Raye Daniels."

Raye sat back down trying to think what to do then remembering what she thought when she found his gun and how she didn't give him the benefit of the doubt. Just then the patio door opened and one of the plain-clothes-men asked to see Gage. Gage waved him over and introduced the tall husky-built man to Raye. "Raye Daniels this is my partner, Eric Williams."

"It's nice to meet you, Raye. Don't be too hard on him; he's actually a great guy once you get to know him. He got lucky doing this job it could have been me."

"I'm the lucky one; he has helped me in so many ways. It's nice meeting you Eric."

Eric smiled, looking at Raye. "There's just one thing we need and that's Mrs. Willoughby's key to search the room."

"I'll get it for you, I'll be right back."

Eric looked over at Gage as Raye went inside. "How's she taking the news?"

"So far better than I thought, she hasn't kicked me out yet or told me to leave."

Eric placed his hand on Gage's shoulder. "You'll be fine bro. She loves you; I saw it in her eyes . . . Oh, and the money in Myles' room, and the numbers you gave me in the envelope, they all matched the Interpol numbers."

"That's great news, but it's too bad for Myles. He's really a nice guy; he's just had some hard times and used poor judgment."

Raye returned with her key, handing it to Eric. "I just thought of something, all those paintings and artifacts around the house, I suppose you'll have to take those as well."

"I'm afraid so, we might need you to tell us where they all are. I will have more people coming tomorrow to go over the place some are experts in their field as well. They can tell forgeries from the real thing, if that's okay with you. I can make it next week if that's better."

Raye looked over at Gage wiping his forehead. "Tomorrow's fine. The sooner it's done the sooner I can rent out the rooms again."

Eric nodded and turned, about to leave. "Oh, I forgot this, it was on Myles' bed. I thought you would like to hang on to it for safe keeping," handing it to Raye. She sat down beside Gage placing it on her lap. It was the sketch book that he had taken with him yesterday and on the front, he had written 'My Family'. Inside were sketches he had drawn of the four of them. Some were group sketches and others were individual sketches. Raye and Gage couldn't believe how beautiful they were. Some were even done in colour.

Ray closed the book and held Gage's hand and looked into his blue eyes. "After everything that has happened, I can't be upset at someone doing their job. I love you and if it wasn't for Mrs. Willoughby and Myles I wouldn't have found you, I could still be with Steve."

"Oh, Steve, I still have his wallet," Gage said out loud.

"His wallet . . . why do you have his wallet?" Raye asked. "No, wait, don't tell me. Anything to do with Steve you can take care of."

Gage placed his arm around Raye holding her close to him giving her a kiss. Raye sat there in his arms feeling secure, thinking of Myles and the other rooms that will be vacant. She looked up at Gage. "I will have to put another ad in the town paper to rent three rooms."

"I don't think I would be in such a hurry to rent out Myles' room and maybe even Mrs. Willoughby's room."

"Why's that?" Raye asked.

"I had a talk with Myles and my captain. I will be vouching for Myles' character and because he turned himself in, they may go lenient with him. The fake Monet hasn't been sold yet plus he only forged one painting, the real one is still upstairs. He also gave back the money and jewels that Mrs. Willoughby gave to him as payment and gifts. He might just get paroled."

"As for Mrs. Willoughby, I'm sure they will go lightly on her after she becomes a witness for the crown prosecutor or makes a plea deal. It was her husband that stole the artifacts, jewellery and paintings from the museum. After he died, she wanted to give it all back but the middlemen saw they could make millions and blackmailed her into keeping it going or they would turn her in as the mastermind, by framing her. Our department has been tracking her for quite some time hoping she would lead us to the others involved."

"That's wonderful," said Raye now knowing that Myles made a good choice and that the man she was in love with was an amazing person. "I guess that means you won't need a place to stay anymore," Raye hesitated, looking at Gage, "now that your job is done."

Gage placed his hand alongside Raye's face and gazed into her alluring green eyes. "I have asked for a transfer to the Turnersfield Police Department. It just so happens that they can use a detective here in town, but

Raye Daniels, I will always be your handyman." Gage pulled Raye into his arms, giving her a passionate kiss letting her know he would never let her go.

About the Author

Sandra Muzyka has a son and a daughter
and six grandchildren. She lives in Ontario, Canada with
her husband, and their two cats. She has been writing
poems and drawing for many, many years as well as
writing children's books. She has put her dreams on
paper for all to see.